THE OFFICE

THE OFFICE

by

JONATHAN GATHORNE-HARDY

HODDER AND STOUGHTON

H25/-

*Printed in Great Britain
for Hodder and Stoughton Limited,
St. Paul's House, Warwick Lane, London, E.C.4.
by Richard Clay (The Chaucer Press), Ltd.,
Bungay, Suffolk*

PART ONE

IN Great Britain there are approximately 4,555,000 office workers. In the United States, 35,391,000; in France, 4,009,481 (this was in 1962); in Germany (1961), 7,065,800; in Italy (1961), 2,697,372.

It was the size of the problem which struck me when I first thought of this book thirteen years ago. I had been in my first office job about eight months. I hated it. Even now, I can remember distinctly the fierceness of my hatred. Often I couldn't stand it. I would go to the lavatory and cry. I would rush out and walk about the streets or go up on to the roof of the huge building I worked in.

It was nothing to do with the people and only partly to do with the job. Practically all work done in offices is trivial and so was this, but it was bearable. The people, with only one exception, were kind and intelligent. My hatred was an almost physical re-action to the sensation of being shut up, every day, all week, in a box; to the cumulative effect of trivial work, to being exposed for the first time to the humiliations, ambitions and restrictions of office life; and to seeing no possible escape from all this for the rest of my life.

I decided that, in the office system, society had created an aberration which it could not control. It was monstrous that I should submit to it. It was monstrous that that huge me—the world—should submit to it.

I began to think about it as the subject for a book. Why had it never been done properly before? The Office in the twentieth century was becoming, not just in terms of numbers, but rela-tively, as important as The Land in the Middle Ages or The Factory in the nineteenth century. Yet there had been no Office Dickens or Office Langland. (I thought then, quite erroneously, that *Piers Plowman* was a fourteenth-century version of an eighteenth-century pastoral hymn to The Land.)

Of course The Office had been used as background or locale in millions of books and plays and films. But it had never been made the hero in quite the way I felt it should. I decided (I was twenty-three) that one day I would write an Epic in which The Office would be the hero (or villain).

NEEDLESS to say, this is not an Epic. I am incapable of writing an Epic (can anyone today?); nor is The Office a suitable subject. But even to make The Office a central character is a problem.

I decided that the solution was to write the book in the form of a film script.

When I read English at Cambridge my tutor Mr. Redpath was always late, sometimes by as much as an hour. In a year of waiting for him I read the collected plays of Sean O'Casey. I noticed, so well known and accepted are the conventions and the appearance of the theatre, that I actually saw a play as I read the words. I was watching the characters from a distance, not moving among them as when reading a novel, or not moving among them in quite the same way. It was a subtle but quite distinct difference of experience.

But how much better known is film. Here the difference in experience becomes even more distinct. The cinema (or television) is an immensely powerful visual medium. It therefore allows you to make any one element—in this case an office—visually overwhelming.

Nor is there any other way of doing this so effectively. Many writers have, of course, borrowed various techniques from films, but unless you actually invite the reader to see a film in his head, you do not get the same emphasis. For instance, you can describe someone looking very closely at his thumb. You can describe the thumb in enormous detail. But how much stronger it is to see it as a film *and* describe it. The camera closes on the thumb. It closes slowly until the thumb fills the entire screen. It holds on the thumb, exploring it, for three minutes. Now, while this giant thumb is towering over the reader's visual imagination, you describe it as well.

3

THERE was a second problem which I thought writing *The Office* as a film script would solve. This will involve a slight digression into the nature of offices themselves.

A book (or film) about an office inevitably has a tendency to be trivial because its ingredients are trivial. It must deal with meetings, typewriters, notes, memos coming round saying that in future all memos will be sent in plastic bags; there are struggles for position but for petty positions, sacrifices but sacrifices for small causes. There are friendships certainly, but nearly always they are one dimensional, they depend for their continuing on the office and not on the characters of the people involved. That is why we so often feel uneasy when we meet our office friends outside the office. I am not saying that strong feelings are not aroused in the office; rat race ambition, fear of the sack, territorial aggression and defence are all strong feelings. But they are not profound or important because the objects and objectives which arouse them are not profound or important. They are trivial.

An illustration of how those engaged in office life instinctively recognise this is office loyalty, the *esprit de corps* that is supposedly one of the deepest and most worthwhile emotions aroused by The Office. In fact—like all office emotions—it is almost instantaneously assumed and as quickly forgotten. Ask any retired businessman how he feels about 'the old firm'. If he left it more than two years before he'll probably ask you what on earth you're talking about. When you explain, he'll say he never gives it a thought. I worked for an advertising agency once. One of our accounts was a brand of cigarette and I remember everyone on the account was put out when a new executive, on his first *day*, talked in glowing terms about one of 'our' campaigns for the cigarette. 'Our'! The cheek of it—he should have said 'your'. But within hours of arriving he already felt 'our', so long had it taken to switch his loyalty from his last agency, identify with the new firm, don *esprit de corps*.

I thought a script might be a way of adding substance to what, I feared, could appear light and somehow unimportant. Making the reader 'see' the office, having it all around him, closing in on him, visually there, endlessly in front of him, might be a method of showing that, although each detail of the office, taken separately, is light, superficial, trivial, combined they form something of enormous size and weight, capable of terrifying destruction.

Whether or not the script does achieve these two things I'm not sure. But I found that when I started to write the book I'd thought about it as a script for so long that it was impossible to write it in any other form.

THE passing of time is one of the hardest things to convey in a film or a book. Just to show or describe ageing, for instance, does not do it. A book is helped by the fact that few people read a book straight through. You are told time is passing. While not reading, the information works in you. (This, incidentally, is one reason 'speed reading'—a book in fifteen minutes—is destructive to literature. The physical time it takes to read a book is one of the elements a writer works with.) In films it is virtually impossible. It is the only area in that most ingenious medium where one has to suspend disbelief. Titling saying 'twenty years later' just evades the issue; the realistic make-up of ageing is never convincing. (Only the long television serial—because it combines the gaps of novel reading with the realism of cinema—achieves a satisfactory sensation of passing time.)

There is no attempt to achieve it in this script. The changing of the seasons therefore has nothing to do with time. It is summer and sunny at the beginning to contrast with the first impression of being shut up in the office. Later, it rains to emphasise this feeling of being trapped. Finally it is winter, dark, snowing, partly to complete the prison of the office (now you can't even look out, or only to see yourself looking in); but the snow also emphasises Peter's view of an office, of its cosiness, its warmth, its safety, its friendliness.

I do, however, want to suggest the effects of time. Though of course people's lives, or wills, are sometimes broken in an office by sudden brutal onslaughts, on the whole the force is cumulative, the result of year after year after year of trivia and routine. It is a Chinese water torture wearing away the skull. Time is the most important dimension in The Office.

5

As first planned, the lavatory was to play quite a major part in the script of *The Office*. It is a definite, if minor, thread, melody, memory in office life.

As I have said, when I first joined an office I remember the lavatory (like Lawrence Gurney in the script) as one of the only places I could hide to regain my equilibrium. Much of the gossip takes place in the women's lavatory. And even in the men's there are embarrasing exchanges, heavy *badinage*. There are some people you only see in the lavatory. You can tell something from the minute rituals (shaken crossed fingers, spitting) they surreptitiously carry out to ward off the evil eye or primitive contagion they obscurely feel they may catch by peeing where someone else has pee'd. You can tell something, or think you can, from whether they wash their hands, or don't, or comb their hair, or whistle, from the way they stand and shake themselves.

Ten years ago I had to write a series of articles about mental illnesses and their treatment. Among others, I used to talk to an extremely intelligent psychiatrist called Michael who worked then at the Maudsley Hospital in London. We would meet in a pub and drink beer while I asked him questions. One evening I noticed while we were peeing that he held his cock in what I called the overhand position. That is, with the thumb underneath and the forefinger and middle finger over the top, sheltering or hiding it. I, on the contrary, held mine in the underhand position, that is with the middle finger underneath and the forefinger resting lightly on top, the same way I hold a cigarette.

When we sat down again I pointed this out. I said I'd frequently noticed this difference at school and in the army. I had sometimes wondered whether it was a class distinction, his way being lower class, mine upper. On the other hand, those who held their cocks in the overhand position, also held cigarettes and knives in the same concealing way. Could it be the result of some puritan instinct—either passed down by copying a father or inherent in the person—to hide the object giving pleasure, whether cock, cigarette or knife?

By an extraordinary chance, Michael not only knew exactly what I was talking about but had noticed the same thing himself. It had interested him so much that before taking his degree he had decided to do a thesis on it. But after several months' research he had come to the conclusion that there was no significance in it. Neither class nor character played any part. It was just one of those random differences, almost certainly passed down through families, for which it was impossible to find any rational explanation.

In my first thoughts about the script, there was going to be

11

greater emphasis, via the lavatory, on this side of male life. I say male—but is it really male, or is it only relevant to those, like me, who have been to, and been slightly warped by, prep schools and public schools? Apart from homosexuals, do memories and knowledge about cocks play such a part in the pasts of all men? I can remember the war between Roundheads and Cavaliers at my prep school. Cavaliers were those who had not been circumcised, so called from the flowing nature of their foreskins. Roundheads had been circumcised and (fortunately, since I was one) were more numerous. This concentration continued until I was about sixteen, so much so that certain cocks (though my relationships with their owners has been entirely chaste) are emblazoned on my mind. For example, there is a man who was my near contemporary at public school. Now he is a distinguished journalist, indeed almost a public figure. Yet when he appears on television, which he does frequently, before I can listen to him, I sometimes glimpse, and then suppress, a startlingly vivid picture of his private parts, of a rather long but narrow cock, with a bold, high-growing, shield-shaped wedge of black pubic hair rising dramatically above it.

Not all chaste, now I come to think of it. When I was nine, at my prep school ('just like puppies y'know. No harm in it. Just puppies.') we used to get into each other's beds and masturbate each other. One boy—R—was particularly advanced and used frenziedly to hiss rather odd things into my ear. I saw him again the other day, at the Aldeburgh Festival. He was in charge of recording, I think, for the BBC or ITV or one of the big Record Companies. Anyway, very important. But when I saw him, all I could hear was—'Smash your balls on a marble slab, smash your balls on a marble slab.'

Originally, the script was going to show the cocks of all the male characters. The viewer would learn, or think he was learning, something about them from their different appearance— just as one learns something, as I have said, from all the things one sees people doing in the lavatory. I also thought this would be a way of showing those elements of homosexuality which are present in offices as in all institutions.

But of course—it was ridiculous. Even before I began to write, I realised that the sight of all those cocks flashing about the screen would have a startling, unbalancing, even mad effect. The lavatory therefore plays the muted and genteel part that no

12

doubt it should. Nevertheless, I want a fragment, a minute echo, of what it might have been, and what it is to some people, to remain . . .

6

THE nature of offices. Their monotony. Nothing new ever happens, every discussion, every drama, every innovation has happened before. But this might be bearable if there was a rhythm, a series of peaks or climaxes. But there isn't; there is no harvest once a year, no play produced after weeks of rehearsal, no child. Or to put it another way, there are a whole series of plays, of children, all of identical importance. An office may grow bigger or smaller with the success or failure of its business, but the rows, the dramas, the events are all the same, about the same things, and after five years or so you realise that neither the crises nor the achievements are of any moment. They are waves on a sea, not foothills leading to a summit.

This monotony is increased because shared. While office events are taking place round you, identical events are taking place in hundreds of thousands of offices in London, France, America, all over the world. An invisible pall of office activity hangs over one, exerting a continuous exhausting, psychic pressure. And the sense of number, spread across the world, makes the office seem part of the human condition, something from which it is impossible to escape.

7

CITIES are jungles. Slowly we learn their lore. I remember the slightly unpleasant feeling it gave me to discover about six years ago that quite unconsciously I always got on to Underground trains at a point which meant I'd be opposite the Exits when I got off.

In the summer, London pubs sweat beer. You can wind them several hundred yards up a street. Or the jungle way people hand themselves along the tops of buses; elbows, knees, handbags, umbrella handles, all gripping, pushing, balancing—expert as the Banderlog.

13

I was on the platform at Victoria last year, catching by chance a Commuter train. For some reason the train was, apparently, a different colour from usual, it was also made of aluminium. The Commuters didn't like it. They shifted and muttered together like old buffaloes at a water hole sensing something wrong. They refused to believe the porters that it was all right, and eventually a special announcement had to be made over the loudspeaker confirming, as it were, that their train was their train.

Never judge girls from the back, from the promise of long hair or legs. Look at the faces of the men approaching them and from their reactions plan your own. (The camera, incidentally, should show Ritson doing this when he sets out at lunchtime for the Hotel Regina.)

And the routes one takes to work or other regularly visited places. These are not necessarily the quickest or shortest, but we take them because we have always taken them. Not to take one of the usual routes causes considerable anxiety. I have often turned abruptly round in mid new route and scurried thankfully back to old route. If London were a jungle, our routes would be where they'd set traps for us—successfully.

All these habits—because that is what the repeated exercise of our jungle lore becomes—are of course useful. The point of habit is to remove from the area of decision as many more (or less) important functions as possible. If we clean our teeth at the same time every morning and evening we don't have to waste time wondering whether we have cleaned them or not, whether we should clean them, how often, and with what. Habit is an automatic pilot freeing the mind for anything else it cares to do.

But there is more to it than this. It is often actually pleasurable carrying out a habit—or can be. The worn paths enjoy being followed, as though nature, realising the importance of habit, had made its exercise rewarding. Because the maths master has made his joke about the eternal triangle two thousand times doesn't mean he won't make it with just as much pleasure the two thousand and first time.

It is this fact, that repetition can bring pleasure, which introduces a soothing element into office events. Since they are enjoyable just because they are repeated, the office worker can, contrary to, or as well as, what I said earlier, have a sense of rhythm. Not just the reappearance of the Christmas party, the annual accounts, the turning on of the central heating—to take some

14

major rhythms. But minute rhythms like the slow breathing of the In Tray, emptying and filling, filling and emptying; every Tuesday a new towel in the Gentlemen's from Rent-a-Towel; the twice-weekly arrival of more stationery; the morning ritual of asking your secretary who's rung, and for her, the ritual of telling you.

8

OFFICES provide security. But this truism conceals a rather curious paradox.

More than most social units, offices are founded on fear. This fear operates outside and inside. Outside, offices fear other offices. They fear competition and takeover, they are afraid their products will become out of date, or that they themselves will. As a result they grow bigger and bigger to fight more effectively. Or smaller and smaller, desperately struggling, till they disappear. They diversify. They call in management consultants or indulge in ruthless purges. Even when they've grown so big and so diverse they haven't any rivals, they are still afraid. The Gas Industry is afraid of the Electrical and Coal Industries and the Government. ICI is afraid of Dupont and of itself (very large, near monopolistic organisations are always afraid of the inertia of their size. Quite rightly.).

But this tendency to grow—here, as elsewhere, the distinguishing mark of our century—of course makes an office still more frightening to those inside it. If my huge office is capable of smashing or defending itself against those other huge offices, what is it not capable of doing to me? Size leads to impersonality and eventually, for most of the inmates, invisibility. 'Morning, Martin,' the Chairman says. 'Henry sir,' murmurs Henry inaudibly, although he's been there ten years and is expected to be on the board in two more. However convincing their contract, no-one in an office feels they may not be sacked tomorrow. Indeed more. When Lawrence Gurney, in the script, is called up to see Ellroyd he not only thinks he is about to be sacked; somewhere deep inside himself he senses Ellroyd may be going to kill him. When a little man is found concealed in the Ladies' lavatory, seven-tenths of the women think, or feel, he had concealed himself there to rape them.

15

In the 1968 floods a man called Spencer in the firm I was with worked late. He left for home, Lewes in Sussex, after a quick light dinner, at about 9.30. The rain poured down, Spencer drove, as usual I imagine, with immense care. Repeatedly he changed course to avoid floods, inching his way nearer home. Eventually, at about 2.30, he realised that if he continued, though he would reach his home in the end, he would be very late at work the next day. He therefore turned round and fought his way back through the floods and storm, arriving at 8.15. All next day he wore his white face, his exhaustion, like a medal. 'Look, sir, how good and conscientious I am.'

The point of this story, however, is not to demonstrate the strength of Spencer's fear, but of his relief. The inconvenience of his drive was nothing compared to the pleasure he got from demonstrating that he was an enthusiastic worker. There are, of course, many strands of fear at work in an office, but one whole part of these expresses itself, as it were in reverse, by the relief at being secure. The feeling of security in the office is in fact a sort of fear, a feeling of insecurity.

9

WHAT effect does The Office have on people after a long time?

I keep on thinking of Anne.

Anne was a woman of about thirty-three or thirty-four in the advertising agency I have already referred to. We shared a room. She had been pretty, and still was when she didn't drink too much beer. She was intelligent, very kind, rather shy. She was sympathetic and amusing to be with.

Over the years I got to know her quite well. She was having an up and down affair with a rather rough journalist—mostly down. She had been a copywriter with the agency for thirteen years, the last six of which had been spent writing copy on lorries. It was a difficult job. Great unwieldy chunks of words, technical terms, whole ready-written phrases and sacrosanct sentences which had to be incorporated. Sometimes she would come back from meetings and I would see her crying at her typewriter, either at some discouraging remarks made about her copy, or about the journalist. Both probably.

I became aware that she was being very gradually ground away.

16

It was not just that I could see the work was hard and unpleasant and could imagine it would grind. I was also able to observe it, to see the damage. She would have good days, happy evenings in the pub when she would be as she must often have been before I came to the firm. These grew less frequent. Or rather the pub evenings grew more frequent, but Anne would drink too much and become miserable or aggressive. Days passed when she would be almost entirely silent in the office. She would attack her type-writer, banging out about lorries. She would pretend not to care what they said about her copy or alternatively care too much, take exaggerated offence. Then she would be happy again, but the gap would have been longer.

I left. I heard about her again about three years ago. There had been some sort of *putsch* at the agency. Anne had been sent to some minor outside branch of it to do business copy—Company reports, Unit Trusts, Institutional prestige I suppose.

She'll be all right. She'll still be paid, have her pension, and, once you've written copy on lorries for six or seven years, adver-tising life has little more that can hurt you. But I still cannot bear thinking of that grinding down, that reduction.

Or take Cyril Wells in the script. His anxiety over his work is so acute that he is only really at ease when he is in the office, because only then can he be sure that nothing is going wrong. In the same way the children from unhappy homes, with separated or quarrel-ling parents, are always more homesick than other children be-cause they are frightened what may happen when they are away.

Or there was a man who used to live next door to me. He was about sixty-seven, with a red, smooth face and hesitant movements. He had retired. He was very proud of having retired. 'Good morn-ing,' he'd say. 'Off to work? No more nine to five for me, thank goodness.' Or 'I can't say I'm sorry to leave the rat race, I really can't say I'm sorry.' Yet he did nothing at all. I studied him. He never went out, his garden was in chaos, often I would think the house was empty, so silent did it look. He did the pools—once an envelope with £1 10s. 0d. was delivered to me by mistake. And once a fortnight he'd take his blue Consul for a short spin to the garage and back. But this upset him. He could never park it again. He'd inch in and out, engine roaring, growing redder and more fussed, getting out to see how far he was from the pavement. When eventually he was within what he no doubt thought was some legal maximum he'd get out and walk slowly round the Consul, testing each door, rubbing off specks, peering at it. I used to have the impression he was somehow filing the car.

10

AFTER years in an office, my neighbour could no longer make up his own mind. He had ceased, to a degree, to be an individual.

In a fascinating book published in 1953, Ralph Partridge gives an account of the history and institution of Broadmoor. I remember hearing him describe (an incident he did not use in the book) a visit to one of the most violent of the inmates. This was an extremely aggressive psychopath who, when he had first arrived, and in fact for many years, had to be forceably restrained by three men whenever anyone entered his cell. Ralph, rather apprehensive, asked if it was safe to go and see him. 'Oh yes,' said the Superintendent. 'He's quite all right now.'

They arrived. The male nurse accompanying them opened the door. Ralph peered in. He saw a very large man of about eighty. His shoulders were shrunken and sunken. He clenched two bony hands between his knees.

'Now then ——,' said the Superintendent, 'how are we this afternoon?'

The old man looked up without speaking. Then suddenly he threw both hands out at them as hard as he could and for a moment the cell was filled with hundreds of little bits of paper and specks of fluff and dust.

The nurse shut the door.

'That's all he does now,' said the Superintendent. 'Spends his whole time tearing up bits of paper, making a sort of confetti, collecting bits of dirt, and then when anyone comes in he throws it at them.'

Of course it would be absurd to suggest that you or I will end our days tearing up memos and flinging the pieces around. Nevertheless, day after day of doing almost the same thing, in the same room, the same building, among the same people, using not one-fiftieth of our brains, whole areas lying inactive and stagnant and slowly dying, stifling all longings and ambitions until they too die, allowing others to take our decisions, or taking them in committees, or else taking them automatically, because the same ones have been taken so often before, so that in fact they are no longer decisions at all—all this, and more, as it goes on for thirty or forty years, does in the end destroy. Not totally of course—prick an old office worker and he bleeds, pinch him and he squeaks—but all of them, all of us, are, in varying degrees, dead.

11

NO-ONE ever seriously believes that they will be in an office *all their working lives*. For forty-five years. Secretly they believe something will rescue them—a football pool, arson. 'I'm sorry, sir. Yes, completely burnt to the ground. As you see sir, just a gaping hole. Not a hope of it starting up again I'm afraid. All the files gone, the records—the whole Board consumed in the flames too I'm afraid. But I understand they were well insured, very well insured. Compensation should amount to three-quarters full salary for the rest of each employee's lifetime. Yes—quite sure, sir. Oh thank you, sir. Good morning, sir.'

Or think of those moments when, quite unexpectedly, you have to leave your office in the middle of the morning. Is it not incredible how violent the feeling of relief is, how fierce, how wild, how irresponsible you feel? You bounce on to buses and into taxis, you could sing or shout, the streets seem filled with massed bands of girls (or young men) all as happy and cheerful and released as you.

Nor of course is it only—or even mostly—the lower echelons of The Office who react like this. Four years ago a survey was made among two thousand directors of British companies. Over 75% said that their main ambition was to retire, and over 65% said that they felt their time at work was wasted. Most of these felt they would be better employed playing golf.

As I said earlier, have you ever spoken to someone who has actually done his term, his whole forty-five years? It is very odd. People who have done that *never refer to it*. Forty-five years of activity has passed and left no trace—or virtually none, an anecdote or two, a brief reference. And in fact you'll find that to them it didn't feel like forty-five years. It felt more like ten.

Another side of the curious perishability of The Office in time is how quickly people are forgotten once they have left. In six months, no-one remembers their names. One or two of course are

19

remembered—I remember Anne—but for every three remembered, two hundred are forgotten. And no-one haunts an office. Factories have ghosts. Not offices.

12

OFFICES are nearly always inefficient. The larger they are the more inefficient. Why is this?

It may be that man is just an inefficient animal. Parkinson, in one of his facetious books, deduces the laws of office inefficiency —work increasing to fit the number of men employed and so on.

I am always reminded of the *Ancien Régime* in eighteenth-century France. De Toqueville was one of the first writers to show that it was the inefficiency of the *Ancien Régime* that was a major cause of the French Revolution. An efficient despotism is terrifying, invincible, an inefficient one can be overthrown. Inefficiency allowed revolutionary ideas to spread and take hold. In the end, inefficiency made inevitable first the financial collapse, and then the initial concessions, both of which led directly to the Revolution itself.

Inefficiency is always on the side of freedom. Even in Russia, bureaucratic lumbering must have preserved many from the machine of State. So too in Spain and Portugal. Inefficiency is almost the only way in which men who are not free can express their desire for freedom, the way in which they can delay evil laws, frustrate their working, mitigate their effects. Inefficiency is a sign that something is wrong—whether it be wild-cat strikes or the way Russian biologists lag behind those in the West.

I often wonder whether the tendency to inefficiency in large office organisations isn't something of the same sort, a secret and, I think, sometimes actually unconscious statement by those who work in them that they want to be free. A tiny rebellion.

13

And so off we set, all of us, our exhausts pluming like stallions, driving through the dawn mist of carbon dioxide, the city haze, taking our usual route and then, finding it crowded, darting down

20

a side street, outwitting, outflanking, out-driving our competitors and brothers—oh it's fun this jungle battle, this ingenious, cunning struggle to get, as quickly as you can, to somewhere you don't want to go.

Why do we do it?

Doesn't that feeling of mingled dread, and pleasure at placating the source of the dread, which we feel on arriving each day remind you of school? And, if of school, also of your childhood?

Because the final, and perhaps the most fundamental, thing about the office is that we are satisfying and placating old schoolmasters, we are hurrying to answer long-silent bells, behaving as long-dead mothers or now-old fathers wanted us to behave. We want and *need* to placate them. They continue to live in us. It calms us to satisfy them. *That* is the source of our relief when we arrive on time—or alternatively of our excitement, our sense of rebellion or guilt when we arrive late.

It is this—this base of unassimilated childhood, of failure to grow up—from which The Office in the end derives its awful authority. The Directors, the Associate Directors, the Group Leaders, the Under Managers, the Liftman, everyone, finds that they both have to behave like, and succumb to, the figures they obeyed so long ago.

14

WHAT are my credentials? The shortest spell I have had in an office was one and a half years. Then there was a term of just over two years. The longest is nearly eleven years, a sentence which I am still serving. My principal satisfaction if this book was a (financial) success, would be that those long years had in the end been the cause of their own destruction.

Not that I want to give the impression that they have been years of unmitigated misery and torture. I have trundled through them like most people, I imagine, occasionally striking blocks of depression or fear or elation, but for the most part tolerating a long, even not unpleasant greyness.

Or so I thought until, as a result of my father-in-law's death last year, I had a rather curious experience.

My father-in-law was supposedly a near millionaire. For a week after he died, fantasy spiralled. By the end of the week I had decided it could hardly be less than £90,000, and might well be a

21

great deal more. I had difficulty sleeping at night, and used to wake up at three or four in the morning, calculating.

But the oddest effect it had was on my behaviour in the office. I kept on losing my temper with my colleagues. Once again I dreaded getting out of bed to go through the rigmarole of the walk, the Underground, the arrival. I found it difficult to sit at my desk for more than quarter of an hour without walking restlessly out, into other offices, corridors, lavatories. Feelings which I remembered from thirteen, fourteen years before suddenly surfaced again, not, as I had thought, changed by the years into resigned acceptance, even a sort of passive enjoyment of my office state, but as fierce and miserable as they had ever been. I thought—I can't stand another week of this.

I stood another week, by which time a letter arrived from my wife's solicitors. My father-in-law had apparently been rather extravagant during the last years of his life, there was death duty on this trust, estate duty on that trust ... the upshot was that there was in fact far less money than anyone, in their worst nightmares, had ever imagined, and we might get £3,000, or perhaps £4,000.

And to my amazement almost at once my office behaviour returned to normal. The feelings of rage and waste sank out of sight again; it had been an uprising of ghosts, a phantom guerrilla force of freedom fighters appearing at night in Czechoslovakia or Spain or South Africa, and vanishing at the break of day.

15

FINALLY, it goes without saying that the script of *The Office* is a comedy. It's often very funny working in an office. Very funny indeed.

PART TWO

A list of the main characters appears on page 128.

THE ARRIVAL

WE are outside Warwick Avenue Underground station. It is about eight thirty in the morning; a fine, fresh day. A Tuesday. We watch people hurry down into the station.

Now the camera joins them, hurrying down the steps, queuing for tickets.

It is important at this stage, and in fact until almost the end of this first section—The Arrival—that all the current clichés of documentary are employed: hand-held camera, wild track, the camera a part of the crowd and so on. Indeed, so strong are the clichés (except that there is no music) that we keep on expecting to hear a commentary.

Down the escalator. Grey faces, already reading their papers. A pretty girl. The advertisements.

We are on the platform. Nothing happens.

All at once the 'Way Out' sign begins to swing very gently. Women's skirts and hair stir. The Underground is breathing. Quite unconsciously, because they have done it so often, unaware that they have absorbed this bit of jungle lore, everyone begins to shift about, looking up for the train, moving into an advantageous position (for some reason they all move down the platform, that is in the direction the train will be travelling, as though the best seats were in the front).

We now hear the train. It roars in. As the doors open, a voice comes over a loudspeaker.

—VOICE: Let them off first, please. Let them off first. Pass right down inside the train. Right down. Let them off first, please.

The train is packed. No-one gets off. Quite the reverse—it looks as though they wish to prevent anyone getting on. We are among the crowd fighting to get in.

And now the camera closes and holds for the first time on a single face. It is Lawrence Gurney. He is forty-two, lined, tired; the lines about the mouth are beginning to give his face, in repose, a slightly bitter expression. (How long does it take a face to adjust to the character inside? How many thousands, hundreds of thou-

25

sands of times must one make an expression before it leaves its permanent trace?)

Lawrence allows himself to be shoved and jostled into the middle of the crowded train. He lifts his head momentarily from his paper, which he has somehow managed to continue reading, and glances over the scene.

The doors close. The train starts to move.

＊　　＊　　＊

We are outside Charing Cross Underground station, at the Villiers Street entrance. The emerging, hurrying crowd—heads up, tucking papers into bags or under arms—immediately fans out up Villiers Street, left under Hungerford Bridge, right into Embankment Gardens. The echoing rumble of the trains carrying further loads of office workers into Charing Cross Railway station above us.

The camera picks on a tall, spare, elderly woman and follows her as she walks briskly through the Embankment Gardens, gradually closing on her.

It is Miss Hockin. She has an inscrutable, stern face, rather like Ivy Compton-Burnett. Her hair is short and greying, her clothes cheap but well kept. She is fifty-two and has been a secretary for thirty-one years.

The camera has closed on her and we now see the gardens through her eyes. It is a day fairly far into summer (say 16th July); the trees are thick with leaves, in the flower beds Geraniums, Agathia, Ageratum, Golden Moss, Tobacco, Aluthum, Fuschia.

Two things are evident from the way Miss Hockin (or rather the camera) looks at the garden: first, that she is a keen gardener; second, that she knows these gardens very well. She may even like pretending they belong to her. Both are illustrated when she stops and stoops to look closely at a Geranium fallen away from its stick. She takes a length of wool out of her bag and ties the flower and stick together again.

Cut to Miss Hockin arriving through the large, open, double, glass and bronze main doors of the office.

Charlie, the liftman, is standing passively beside one of the three automatic lifts. Miss Hockin smiles at him briefly.

—CHARLIE: Mornin'.

26

Miss Hockin joins six other people in the lift. The doors shut.

*   *   *

The camera follows the progress of the lift on the indicator. When it reaches the tenth and top floor the camera continues to move up the wall, as though following the lift some invisible floor higher.

Cut to outside and above the office. We are sufficiently high above it to see in the workers hurrying across Waterloo Bridge, along the Embankment and the Strand, around the Aldwych, up and down Kingsway, patterns of convergence on to the various huge office blocks in that area.

Sufficiently high above it, as well, not to be certain from which one we have just emerged. Throughout this film, though we know the rough area, we never know accurately where the office is. It could be the old Shell building, the BBC's Bush House, Rediffusion, Somerset House . . . there are at least four dozen offices in that square half mile it could be. Later on, when we look out of the office windows, the views we see should be shot from as many different buildings as possible in this district, deliberately to add to the confusion. The supposition is that the office is so large it covers the whole area.

In the centre of the camera's view a Rolls-Bentley is crossing Waterloo Bridge. We follow it over the lights and up Kingsway.

The camera zooms down. The Rolls has stopped. We watch Woodrow Bolton, the Chairman, step briskly out and briskly run up the steps through the high, glass and bronze doors.

Woodrow Bolton is sixty-four though he looks fifty (nothing reveals his age; even his teeth are small and neat). He is five foot three, with bulbous eyes, fuzzy eyebrows, a short, thick neck covered in bristles, a faint but hard to define air of alcohol about him and a diffident, irascible manner.

As he comes towards the lift, some ancient memory of discipline stirs in Charlie. He shuffles.

—MR. BOLTON: Morning, Charlie.

—CHARLIE: Mornin', sir.

—MR. BOLTON (sniffing): Is there always this smell of onions here?

—CHARLIE: What, sir?

—MR. BOLTON: There definitely is this morning. A not very

27

pleasant smell of frying onions. Have you been busy in some little den?

The lift arrives from the lower ground floor. The five people in it are appalled to see Mr. Bolton. Their faces freeze in various expressions of nervousness, bravado, not noticing who it is, etc. Mr. Bolton steps in, followed by Charlie.

—MR. BOLTON (aggressive shyness): Well, do any of *you* notice the smell of onions?

The lift doors close.

—MAN IN THE LIFT: Where, sir?

—MR. BOLTON: In the hall. Here. Unmistakable.

No-one answers. They all look as though they've just remembered they did, in fact, have onions for supper. Mr. Bolton can be heard breathing. The lift stops at the third floor. Though it is not anyone's floor, everyone gets out except Mr. Bolton and Charlie.

—MR. BOLTON: Fourth floor today please, Charlie. I may catch someone by surprise.

Mr. Bolton's voice and expression have become indifferent. He steps through the doors and says without looking back:

—MR. BOLTON: Do something about those onions, Charlie.

Charlie watches him march briskly down the corridor. The doors close. Charlie, momentarily enlivened, presses the tenth floor button. But someone on the ground floor has already pressed the button there and the lift descends.

*　　*　　*

We descend with it. At the bottom eight people are waiting. Charlie comes out to let them in. The last one, on whom the camera concentrates, is Bob Glenny. He is fifty-five (though looks younger—say, forty-nine), with a brown, wrinkled, aquiline face. He has an air of great calm. He is carrying a large blue canvas bag, zipped shut.

Just as Charlie, holding the doors back from outside the lift, takes away his arm, a young man dashes in. He shouts.

—YOUNG MAN: Hold it, Charlie!

Charlie presses the button, the doors reopen. The young man rushes into the lift, knocking Bob's bag out of his hand.

—YOUNG MAN: Sorry, all.

—MAN IN LIFT: What you got in that bag—lead? It's heavy.

The camera closes on the bag, which has fallen on the man's

foot. Bob Glenny bends and picks it up. In a tone of placid satis-
faction, as though this was the *raison d'être* of the bag.
—BOB GLENNY: I know.
The lift doors close.

*   *   *

We remain with Charlie. He watches the lift's progress on the
indicator. He is a short man, very bent—almost a hunchback.
Fifty. He wears a blue uniform. His face is like that of an embryo,
with hardly any chin or forehead, puffy yellow flesh, blunt little
nose to which, however, the direction of the face tends, if towards
anything.
He goes to the door and stares at a pigeon on the pavement.
The camera closes on the pigeon and then returns to Charlie's
face. We notice a resemblance, though Charlie does not have the
pigeon's alert, intelligent eye.
His day has begun, a day in which, from 9 o'clock until 5.30, he
has absolutely nothing to do whatsoever.

*   *   *

We are in Cyril Wells's suburban kitchen. He is at the table,
swiftly eating Rice Krispies. A small, prematurely grey man of
thirty-four, with Brylcreem and a thin anxious face. He is looking at
a sheaf of papers bull-dog clipped to a board at his left. He mutters
and murmurs, while gobbling and nibbling his Rice Krispies.
His wife is in her dressing-gown, frying sausages at the gas
stove.
—CYRIL (murmuring rapidly): Invoice . . . Bee didn't sign . . .
mmmm . . . first thing . . . mmm . . . report the meeting, then get
. . . mmmm . . . Oh Christ . . . mutter mutter mutter . . .
He clenches his jaw, turns pages, smoothes his Brylcreemed
hair, mutters. A sudden compulsive movement dashes half a
dozen Rice Krispies across a time-table.
—CYRIL: Oh Christ!
He springs up, moves as though to get a cloth, recollects his
tissue, darts back, pulls it, neatly folded, from his waistcoat
pocket and scrubs hard at the time-table.
His wife turns and sees some of this. She is plainly accustomed
to Cyril's anxieties, at the same time she does not despise them.

—WIFE: I'll fold you another tissue.

She does, and tucks it into his waistcoat pocket.

—CYRIL: Yes. No. I—ah—can't remember if Bee, if I *gave* Bee... It's always a *bit* difficult now since... Far more responsibility. Um. No—um—I think I'd best be off. You gave me a tissue...

—WIFE: No sausages?

Cyril puts on his mackintosh, knocks his board off the table, picks it up.

—CYRIL: I'll fill up in the canteen. I'm sure I forgot to tell Bee...

* * *

We are watching Miss Hockin walk down a corridor. Medium shot.

In the same way as the locale of the office is never accurately defined, nor is its appearance. At the beginning, with its large double doors, the automatic lifts and other details, it is a big, expensive, modern, semi-skyscraper office block. But now, as we begin to accompany Miss Hockin, it is much more run down. The linoleum on the floor is a bit cracked, our glimpses into such offices we pass with open doors confirms this. It is possible that the actual quality of the film alters in sympathy, becoming yellower (sepia), more jerky. Later on, when Ritson appears, the office becomes definitely sleazy, the four-roomed business premises of a publisher of pornographic books say. Or rather, that part of the office in which Ritson and Martin live becomes like this.

Miss Hockin turns into another corridor, up some stairs, left at the top, along another worn corridor.

* * *

Quick cut to Lawrence Gurney striding through the Embankment Gardens. The camera exclusively on his face. His rather thin, longish hair bouncing and blowing. He is tense, excited, probably rehearsing a speech or a letter in his head.

* * *

Woodrow Bolton is walking down the smart, executive corridor of the fifth floor. The carpet is thick and mushroom coloured. The doors are labelled with the names of Directors, Company Secretaries and with their titles. On the walls are expensive modern pictures lit by clusters of tiny aluminium spotlights.

Mr. Bolton failed to find anything wrong on the fourth floor. He is not put out. Coming towards him is Janice.

Janice is Lawrence Gurney's secretary. She is nineteen and has a pert, rather arrogant face, long black hair, large, over-emphasised breasts and a loose but pleasing mouth. There is a hint of sluttishness, not yet developed. Her eyes are a bit shifty. You have the feeling that vitamin juices, reinforced foods and male attention have somehow over-stimulated and too-early developed her. It will be several years before anyone—herself included—knows what she is really like.

—MR. BOLTON: Good morning.

—JANICE: Good morning, sir.

Mr. Bolton stops, compelling Janice, out of deference, to stop too. They are, in any case, outside the door of Mr. Bolton's office.

—MR. BOLTON (as though it were on the tip of his tongue): You are . . . You work . . . new?

—JANICE: I'm Mr. Gurney's secretary.

Mr. Bolton walks into his office so that Janice has to follow him.

—MR. BOLTON: Ah yes—Gurney.

His office has three abstract paintings, a Paolozzi sculpture like a barnacle-encrusted mine, a yellow carpet, two Corbusier steel-sprung chairs, a black leather-covered table, bare but with concealed electronic dictating and communication equipment, and a lot of invisible but powerful lighting which is all on, despite the sun pouring through the double-glazed windows and long Terylene-muslin curtains which take up the whole of one wall. But although it seems to reveal a fairly definite taste, you would learn little of Mr. Bolton's character from this room. From time to time he changes the decoration entirely—recently, after increasingly short intervals.

Behind the leather-topped table, a door, now shut, leads into the Chairman's suite—a bedroom, bathroom and dining-room.

—MR. BOLTON: Gurney, Gurney, Gurney—let me see. Gurney—now. What is it Gurney does?

31

—JANICE: He's a Group Head. Packaging and . . .

—MR. BOLTON (quickly): Design Group. That's it. One of the Packaging and Design Groups. I thought so. I'd say ambitious. An ambitious kookie. Would you agree?

—JANICE: Oh yes.

—MR. BOLTON: You must have ambition. I used to have it. I've been at the top too long. Ambition can get rusty. Are you ambitious?

Janice is rather uneasy. She looks about her. It is embarrassing being marooned in the middle of a large, yellow carpet. All at once, quite near her feet, her eyes light on a darker patch, a five-inch irregular stain where something has been spilt. The camera rests on this. Then Janice steps, or rather shifts on to it, as though it were an island. This act, perhaps by defining her position, seems to make it more secure.

—JANICE (giving the answer wanted): Yes, I suppose I am in a way. Oh yes, I'd like to do better. I'd like a better position.

Mr. Bolton is now standing rather close to her. He is engaged in his current role. The tycoon who pounces unexpectedly, anywhere, appearing now among the mighty, now at the side of the most humble. Nothing is so trivial that it doesn't hold the germ of something significant. He is breathing rather heavily.

—MR. BOLTON: Would you? Are you? I shall see what I can do. What were you doing on this floor?

Miss Sturt comes briskly in from her adjoining office. She is fifty, competent, plump, motherly. She has been Mr. Bolton's secretary for ten years. When she comes in he steps quickly back.

—MR. BOLTON: Good. Well—well, I'll see what I can do. Now you'd better get back to Gurney.

Janice goes out. Mr. Bolton turns to Miss Sturt. His face is judicious.

—MR. BOLTON: That girl has ambition, Sheila. It just shows the sort of information you can pick up. Do any of the Directors need a new secretary? What about Cameron? Find out if there's any *niche* (he pronounces it nitch) for her.

Miss Sturt has been placing two piles of letters on the black table, one opened, one unopened.

—MISS STURT: Yes, Mr. Bolton.

She goes out. It is evident she has no intention of doing

32

anything. Mr. Bolton stares after her, rising slowly up and down on his toes. He is standing on the stain just vacated by Janice.

*   *   *

The camera rejoins Miss Hockin at the end of the worn corridor. She goes up some stairs, left at the top, along another corridor.

She opens the door and walks into her office. It is a modest twelve by ten foot box which was last decorated four years ago. It has a brown rug in the middle of the dark green linoleum. There is a calendar on the wall, a large steel filing cabinet near the door, an excessive number of potted plants (Busy Lizzie, Wandering Jew, variegated ivys, Sansivana and a rubber plant), a wooden desk by the window, etc., etc.

Miss Hockin takes off her coat and hangs it up. She opens the window wider. She starts to go round the plants. One of these has fallen from its stick and, taking some wool from her bag, she ties it back again. The ritual of arriving in the office.

*   *   *

Bob Glenny, carrying his blue canvas bag, comes into the Design Group studio. He stops at the door to hang up his mackintosh.

There are about a dozen people in the studio, all part of Lawrence's Packaging and Design Group. You can see the Thames through the large windows, flowing huge and eighteenth century about half a mile away.

Bob picks up his bag and feels its weight appreciatively.

—BOB: It's heavy all right. I'd have hardly been likely to bring it in otherwise, would I?

He laughs quite heartily at this inexplicable joke. No-one in the rooms looks up. Bob walks towards his Designer's easel, still chuckling. As he passes close to two other easels he says:

—BOB: Hi, Geoffrey. Morning, Ray.

Ray look up briefly and smiles.

—RAY: Hi, Bob.

Bob is No. 2 in Lawrence's Packaging and Design Group. He was passed over when Lawrence arrived, but has never appeared to mind. He reaches his own easel and once more weighs the bag in his hand. Then he sinks into his chair and begins slowly to fill his pipe.

*   *   *

Peter Villiers is bicycling to work along the Embankment. He is a tall, stooping young man of thirty, who looks a little like the Dauphin in the film *Henry V*. He hums as he bicycles.

At first we think that his eye tends to light on young, good-looking working-class men—because that is what the camera is doing. But we soon realise—for the same reason—that it is in fact attractive young faces of either sex and any class that he likes. He also notices architectural oddities—gables, gargoyles, the dolphins on the lamps along the Embankment.

A series of cuts and dissolves bring Peter inside the office. He moves languidly down the corridor, peering through each open door.

He passes Bee's office. She is at the far end of it, making up her face.

—PETER: Morning, dear.

Bee, her large wrinkled lips pulled smartly back from long yellow teeth, gives him a flashing scarlet smile but immediately continues to apply her lipstick.

Peter turns up some stairs. His office is two floors higher.

*   *   *

Lawrence is by the In Tray in his office, shuffling through the papers in it. The letter or document he wants isn't there.

He comes towards his desk, screwing up his eyes to take in the regular and neat heaps of Packaging and Designing material with which it is piled—sliced plastic sheets, a corrugated mock-up, sketches, plans, etc. All tidy and to hand.

He sits down and picks two of these up, distaste and humorous acceptance on his slightly over-expressive face.

Suddenly, with great weariness, all expressions cease. He sits, his hands resting on a wrapper, with his eyes shut.

*   *   *

We dissolve through to the sleeping face of Ritson. We are in

34

bed with him, a hot, stuffy, steamy, untidy double bed. His thick face is sweaty. His large mouth is open, the lips cracked and rimmed black with the night before's red wine.

He stirs and mutters, feeling in the bed behind him.

—RITSON (muttering, eyes still shut): Where are you?

Realising that whoever it was has got up, he rolls heavily on to his back and looks blearily at his watch.

—RITSON: Christ!

He gets out of bed. He is naked, with a strong, thick body, rather hairy. He is forty-five. He walks over to the basin, scratching his scrotum, yawning, etc. He runs the cold tap into a glass, puts in two Alka-Seltzer, and then puts his head close to the tap and splashes his face.

He comes back and sits on the bed, listening absently to the fizzing in the glass before putting it on the table beside him. He picks up the telephone, dials, waits. Drinks half the Alka-Seltzer.

—RITSON: Geoffrey Ritson, B Sales Manager please. (Pause.) Martin? It's Geoffrey, anything happening? (Pause.) Good Lord, at *eleven*? Look, could you phone his secretary. Say I'm visiting the South London Reps and won't be in till after lunch, could you? I *will* be in actually, when I can pull myself together, probably in half an hour. Hold the fort till then, old cock.

He drinks the rest of the Alka-Seltzer, listening to the phone.

—RITSON: Yes. 'Bye.

He gets up from the bed and goes to the bedroom door. He opens it with his left hand, absently pulling back the curtains of the window with his right hand.

—RITSON (calling downstairs): Angela? Darling? Is there any breakfast left, darling?

From downstairs comes the clatter of breakfast, several children, and Angela calling something we cannot distinguish though Ritson evidently can.

He scratches his scrotum again and comes back into the room. He staggers a little, still half drunk. He veers towards the table and gathers up the glass to give himself more Alka-Seltzer. There is something animal but endearing about him. He's like a randy, middle-aged badger.

*   *   *

Mr. Bolton is standing looking irritably at his list of engage-

35

ments. Miss Sturt, whom he has just called, waits fairly patiently in the door that leads to her small adjoining office.

—MR. BOLTON : Why have I got to see Bee at twelve-forty-five?

—MISS STURT : She asked to see you.

—MR. BOLTON : I suppose I'll have to—if only for old time's sake. She's still a sexy thing—even if she's sixty.

—MISS STURT : Really, Mr. Bolton!

—MR. BOLTON : Well—fifty-five. She must be nearly, you know. Well-preserved woman.

He goes on looking down the list.

—MR. BOLTON : Jack at eleven-thirty. I suppose so—if I'm to learn to delegate. Yes. Um. Why on *earth* have a Board meeting at three o'clock? No-one will be sober. I didn't arrange that.

—MISS STURT : You agreed to it. I asked you . . .

—MR. BOLTON : (interrupting) : I must have been mad. Yes. Um. Yes. Look, Sheila, *please* try and find me half an hour some time in the morning.

He comes round from behind his desk, his hand out appealingly, holding the list for her to rearrange.

—MR. BOLTON : Tell Bee I can only give her ten minutes or something. Put Jack off ten minutes. I must have half an hour. I'm on to something. It may seem small, but you can't have an oak without an acorn. I think I'm on to an acorn. Here's . . . (Fade)

*   *   *

As the vision fades, so does the sound. We hear nothing during this next sequence.

The camera is flowing through the office. It advances soundlessly through filled but silent corridors, in review past all the people (except Miss Hockin) we have so far seen, and all the people we have yet to see. The office settling down.

It moves with increasing speed. Faces blur. Notices blow out from boards, internal windows, frosted, flip past, we flow urgently through the office—a canteen, a silent winking telephone exchange, a room full of typewriters and typists.

The camera has a purpose. It is taking us somewhere. As it slows down we recognise the route; along a worn corridor that we remember, up some stairs, left at the top, along another corridor. And as it slows, the sound begins to return.

36

It comes to rest, with a sense of inevitability, facing the door of Miss Hockin's office.

*   *   *

Miss Hockin finishes watering the last of her plants. She walks over to an In Tray on a table by the door and picks up a bundle of papers and letters. Taking this over to her desk, she rapidly sorts through it, throwing three or four away into a green tin waste-paper basket after a brief glance, and arranging the rest in order.

She puts on a pair of spectacles and carries the pile of papers over to the filing cabinet. She pulls open the bottom drawer and, moving with economy and neatness, steps in and lies down inside it. She lays the papers on her chest.

The camera is inside the filing cabinet drawer. From a position approximately the same as Miss Hockin's head, able to see her feet resting together at the front of the drawer, we see her deftly start to shut it by pulling with her hands on the underside of the drawer above.

The area of light at her feet grows rapidly less. Soon there is a faint click, then silence and darkness.

THE MORNING

LAWRENCE'S office. It is medium smart, with wall-to-wall, somewhat frayed mushroom carpet, no pictures, bookshelf containing eleven books and old Gloy pots, tins of pins, Cow Gum, etc., orange baize board with notes and lists on it, Anglepoise table lamps and a smallish window, with green curtains, through which comes the sun. With him sit Janice, who is typing, and Chris, his small, slight trainee, a would-be Packager and Designer aged about twenty-five.

Lawrence has been holding a plan of some packaging design and staring at it.

—LAWRENCE (slight effort): Oh Chris—here's something you could do—quite a nice little problem to think about.

One of the internal telephones rings. Lawrence reaches for it but is beaten by Janice.

—JANICE: Mr. Gurney's secretary. (Pause.) I'll ask him. (To Lawrence) Bob Glenny wants a word.

—LAWRENCE: OK.

—JANICE: It's OK.

She replaces the telephone and continues typing. Lawrence stares at the display plan, frowning. They wait for Bob, who appears almost at once through the door, thrusting before him a large cardboard mock-up almost the same size as himself, of a Display. It could be for 'displaying' almost anything—an electric cooker, irons, a pile of books, a new cooking oil, soap.

—BOB (talking slowly as he advances with measured steps carrying the Display): I thought I'd have a word with you about the new Unit, Lawrence. I'm not entirely happy about one development. I've had a new notion about it.

Lawrence begins to show exaggerated enthusiasm and interest. He half stands up, waving Bob unnecessarily into a chair.

—BOB: It's a question of these flaps here. With the original design they hang down as you'll remember. That shows everything off, and if you like you can write your message, your slogan, your price offer or what have you on them.

He pauses to take out and start filling his pipe. Lawrence is

38

leaning forward, his face twitching a little. God this is exciting, he seems to be saying, go on, go on. In the background, Janice finishes her typing and leaves the office.

—BOB: Now—I had the notion that if you twisted those two flaps to the side, it would be an advantage. You——

—LAWRENCE (breaking in): —reveal the product even more. *Excellent.* And get your flaps round to the side for extra exposure of the message. I think that's great, Bob. I really do.

—BOB: —can then do something like this.

He bends forward to demonstrate, pipe as revolver.

—BOB: First, you get a nice big space in front for your display. Larger than before. Much larger. Then twist them right to the side—so—and you either have four sides for your little message, or bent back—so—you have additional depth to play with at the sides. I thought, if you'd authorise it Lawrence, of getting a quote on that for the first batch of 18,000.

—LAWRENCE: I think it's just great, Bob. Of course, on the first batch. Chris—come and look at this. You remember I told you that the first rule of Packing and Display was to reveal your goodies—and I'm sure Bob has told you that, he's been in this business far longer than I have—then the *next* stage, what we call *Creative* packaging——

He pauses, with a grimace. Suddenly the process of self-generated enthusiasm seems to falter. He wavers, but it is difficult to say if he's stopped because he was bored by what he was saying, or because he was naturally side-tracked and intrigued by the idea of Bob's long service. They could even be connected.

—LAWRENCE: —leads—doesn't it, Bob?—on from there (pause) in very much the same way. Bob—how long exactly *have* you been here?

—BOB (sitting back again, pipe): Twenty-nine years.

—LAWRENCE: Twenty-nine years! That's more than me. I've been sixteen or seventeen with them—but then I did eight with the branch in Manchester. Do you ever want, do you ever find (pause—head on one side, smiling, expression that is quizzical, frank, honest) that you'd ever like . . .

—BOB (easily, comfortably): Oh, you mean promotion? No, as I told you when you came, Lawrence, I've never been ambitious in *that* sense. To do a good job, ambitious for a good bit of packaging or display. Yes. But not in *that* sense, of power and so on. I'm king in my own home and that's enough for me. Rule your

39

roost and you don't want anything else.

—LAWRENCE : I didn't quite mean that actually. What I meant was doesn't the length of time ever get you down? Don't you sometimes feel, I'm sure I do, I'm sure we all do, that you ought to get out, do something else . . .?

—BOB : Oh, of course I get bored at times. Who doesn't? Routine. But it's secure, of course. I've got my pension now. Not large enough yet—but another few years will help. I'll tell you one thing though, I wouldn't like to do the whole of my time, not till the end. But I'll tell you the secret—I've outside interests, I've got certain expectations. That's what you need. You mean stay till the end—another ten years? No.

—LAWRENCE : Twenty-nine years is quite a long time, Bob.

—BOB : Well, it's relative, isn't it? How long do we live? Seventy-five years? Seventy-nine? My family live into their eighties. Twenty-nine looks pretty small then. No—luckily I've outside expectations. Otherwise I couldn't stand the thought— well, I could stand it—I wouldn't like to think of another ten years. Four or five, yes.

Ray, one of Bob's assistants, puts his head round the door.

—RAY : Could Jessie have a word with you, Bob? She's got some query from Dispatch.

—BOB : Right, then. I'm glad you like the display idea, Lawrence. I'll put it in hand.

He carries out the Display piece. Lawrence has his head in his hands, his elbows amidst package and display. He sits for so long that Chris becomes uneasy. Eventually he goes :

—CHRIS : Is there anything wrong, Lawrence?

—LAWRENCE (looking up with a sweet smile): You know, I realised this morning that I loathe it here. I can't stand it. I hate it more than I've ever hated anything. I despise it. It's driving me mad. I'd like to smash it up.

Peter Villiers comes carefully through the door.

—PETER : Sorry to butt in, Lawrence—could I borrow Janice and Chris for half an hour? A tiny emergency, and Karen's ill.

—LAWRENCE : I suppose so.

He spins his chair violently and stares out of the window.

—PETER : Thank you *so* much. But where *is* Janice?

—CHRIS : She'll be gossiping with Diane. In the telephone exchange.

—PETER : Thank you *so* much, Lawrence.

40

Lawrence doesn't answer or turn round. Peter makes an expression ('oh dear') and he and Chris go out, followed closely by the camera.

*   *   *

Peter and Chris have collected Janice and are walking towards the stairs. As they pass the lift, its door open to reveal Charlie, alone, standing at the back. The lift doors close on him.

Peter, Chris and Janice start up the stairs and disappear off screen.

The camera continues past the lift and begins to close on a door beside which hangs one of the Office Notice Boards. On this are pinned 'Dear All' letters, For Sale notes, Rugby/Football/Cricket teams, Lateness Must Stop notices and so on.

The camera dissolves through the door.

*   *   *

It is the office of the Thumb Man. It is not as smart as Lawrence's, but not as disreputable as Ritson's. It is on a par with Miss Hockin's. The only peculiarity is that it has no windows, only a powerful Vent-Axia machine and a skylight, at the top of a long shaft, which itself only opens on to a well in the building.

Sitting with his back to us is a large man with short grey hair which fringes, almost like a monk, the large and shiny bald top of his head. He is looking at his thumb.

The camera closes on the thumb. It is large and quite ordinary, except for a small piece of dirty Elastoplast wrapped round the top. The camera must hold on the thumb, close, for as long as it takes three people to ascend two flights of office stairs, say, thirty-five seconds.

*   *   *

Peter, Chris and Janice arrive at the fifth floor. As they pass the lift, its doors open to show that it is empty except for Charlie. He leaves it, crosses slowly to the lift opposite. He presses the button and stands waiting.

They take no notice, but continue past the lift down the corridor and into Peter's office. This is much the same as Lawrence's, but has some personal touches.

—PETER: Oh dear, I hope I didn't offend.

—JANICE (laconically, almost bored): His wife's left him again.

—PETER: I know, dear. And how did *you* know?

—JANICE: He threw all their furniture out of the window. Smashed the lot. I overheard him on the telephone. Well, you can't help it. I think he wants me to hear. It gives him a kick. He goes right on in front of you. How did you know, come to that?

—PETER: I can't remember. I simply seem to absorb information like that out of the air by a sort of osmosis.

—CHRIS: Actually I think he's worried by his work. I don't think he really likes it. As far as I can gather.

—JANICE: Who does?

—PETER: Now, dear, it really is rather urgent. Janice, could you be an angel and type these five letters and then a meemo, dear? They were in Karen's shorthand but I've written them out for you. And don't forget a plastic bag for the meemo, dear.

Janice exits, everything tilted, pouting, swinging. Any trip down the corridor is an adventure. Who will see her, who will she see?

—PETER: And, Chris—I'd go myself but I've a meeting. Could you take these specifications down to the Patent Office. Ask for a Mr. Jarrett and he'll check them for you. I've rung him. I have a terrible feeling we're about to break copyrights, patents and goodness knows what else.

As Chris nods and goes out, Peter calls.

—PETER: Take a taxi both ways. Charge it.

Peter reaches for the telephone, dials, speaks.

—PETER: I've got a moment or two, dear. Can I come and gossip?

*   *   *

Five quick cuts which, superficially matching, appear to establish a relationship which does not exist.

Bee making up her face again.

Charlie slumped in his chair beside the front door lifts.

The Thumb Man. He is still staring at his thumb, but is tensed and hunched, as though listening for something or waiting to be shot. The Elastoplast has been removed, revealing nothing.

Lawrence savagely turning everything out of the In Tray.

Last, Bob Glenny peeing at a stand-up in the Gentlemen's, that

42

echoing, cracked grotto. He pees rather elaborately, with a lot of knee-bending and shaking, whistling loudly. One lavatory door is shut (four others open). When he has finished, Bob looks quickly round then, still whistling, bends to see beneath the door. There are two feet. He straightens, washes his hands, walks out. He is smiling.

*　　*　　*

Bee's office is a little bit grander than Peter's, but only because she has wrested various privileged objects—two pictures, two waste-paper baskets, an armchair, a standard lamp, etc.—from the Office Manager. Her feminine hand is heavy, chiefly evident in 'treasures' brought from home: a huge spray of Constance Spry spouting from a large cut-glass vase, a headscarf from Portofino over the filing cabinet, a photograph of her and her first husband on a bookshelf, herself and her second husband on the desk. She is never sure whether the pleasure of boasting about her husbands is outweighed by the impression of bad taste it might give, so the photograph of her and her third husband is on its back on a small bookshelf by her left elbow. Not visible but within reach.

Peter comes through the door and bends into the armchair, crossing his legs. Looking into her hand-mirror, Bee rolls her lips over each other to spread the lipstick.

—BEE (still rolling lips): Mmmm—must tell you—mmm—funny thing—mmm—so typical of—mmmm—Jack. That's better. Sorry. No, it was Jack Ellroyd. You know, after all these years, I have managed to get myself, well, a 'special position' in the firm, don't you? One of the little things I sometimes do, outside my Advisory capacity of course, is little leaflets and so on. I spent a year as a journalist, as you know. I'd *done* one of these, oh weeks ago. Something they could send round with that new project—whatsitsname? You know. How it ever got to Jack Ellroyd I can't imagine. Bolly sometimes sees my things—I send them to him. But, Jack—especially since his elevation . . . *Any*way, in he swep' this morning, oozing charm from every pore. He *is* a very attractive man. I must say this for him—he went to the point at once. 'Bee, darling' (never called me darling in his life!) 'Bee, darling—just reassure me about this first sentence.' He was holding my leaflet—well it was a *booklet* really, a small book. I was dumbfounded.

43

—PETER: What was the first sentence?

—BEE: The best in the book. 'My hot plates satisfy my needs.' Bang on.

—PETER: 'My hot plates satisfy my needs?'

—BEE: Yes. I'd written it as if by myself, using my own name, with a photograph of myself. The personal is always more interesting then the impersonal—an old journalists' trick. I have a small reputation in that field as well.

—PETER: Your (pause) . . . needs. I suppose dear . . .

—BEE (not listening): I'm afraid I had to put Jack Ellroyd firmly in his place. I explained that after all these years I *had* got—well, a 'special position' in the firm, I *did* know what I was talking about. I said that if he liked I'd discuss it with Bolly. In fact I'm going to have a word with Bolly about it this very morning. Well, in the end, out he had to swep' again, still oozing charm from every pore!

—PETER: Goodness.

Alaister appears at the door, with a highly nervous Cyril Wells jostling and pushing behind him.

—ALAISTER: I'm sorry—are you busy? I can come back.

—BEE: No, no—only nattering. Come in. Join the *Salon*.

Alaister comes in, followed by Cyril anxiously holding his board, bull-dog clip and papers like a tray in front of him.

—CYRIL: I wonder—ah—sorry to barge in Bee—just a quick word, a check—ah—there may have been a bit of a bog-up, that is clog-up, in the system . . .

—BEE (interrupting): What is it?

—CYRIL: Sorry, Peter. Now (shuffling through papers) can you remember, I have no record, did you get a memo yesterday?

—BEE: What memo?

Cyril spies two Rice Krispies caught between his papers. Nervously he pops them into his mouth.

—CYRIL (munching): Well that's our problem. Without a record of course I've no means of knowing. That *is* a flaw in the system. If I'm not sent a record, then we've no means of *telling*.

—BEE (exasperated, impatient to make the most of her salon while it holds together): For goodness sake, Cyril, it can't be that important. Yes, I did get one. Now, I've an important meeting on.

—CYRIL: Oh good. You're sure? A memo yesterday? Splendid —that is if you're sure?

—BEE: Yes, yes, quite sure.

—CYRIL (backing out): Ah—sure—splendid—good . . .

—BEE: Honestly the fuss they make—what with plastic bags, signing for memos . . . Now where were we? I don't think you two have met, have you?

—PETER (rising): No, I don't think we have.

—BEE: Alaister. Trainee, doing a tour. A very bright painter. Interested in the theatre. Comes from Wiltshire. Twenty-four. Peter. Age unknown. In Specifications. Tremendous gossip. Knows all about the ballet. There—I always think I'm rather good at 'instant thumbnails'. It's so necessary to give people the 'essentials'.

Pause.

—BEE (with a gush of enthusiasm): Oh, but I must tell Alaister about my little brush with Jack Ellroyd. You won't mind, Peter—you're such a good listener—don't go. *Any*way, Alaister, as you know, after all these years I *have* managed to get myself, well, a 'special position' in the firm. One of the little things I do, outside my Advisory capacity naturally, is a booklet now and then. I was a journalist once . . .

But Peter manages to steal away, followed by the camera. Bee, of course, observes him going out but just gives him a gay and gracious wave—there's no compulsion in the world of the salon —and turns with redoubled energy upon Alaister.

*   *   *

Outside, in the corridor, what one may call the Wild Track of the office continues. It is to be understood that this continues throughout the film. That is, there is the perpetual clatter of typewriters, conversations are interrupted by telephone calls— 'Hullo . . . yes . . . on Wednesday? . . . four thirty in the third Conference Room . . . all right'—boys come in with pieces of paper and put them in In Trays, and remove other bits of paper from Out Trays, people sing and whistle; tunefully or tunelessly—'Give a lit-ill, whis-ill, give a lit-ill, whis-ill—whoo whee, whoo whee— whis-ill.' The unit that makes the film must employ a whole army of extras whose sole job is to reproduce the incessant ant-like movement, the continual bombardment of minute but grinding noise, which constitute the environment of an office.

At the same time, the film must achieve in an hour what an

office usually requires some years to do. That is the effect of being stifled, crushed, buried.

How to achieve it? For one thing, from now on the camera should always glance at the ceiling as it passes down corridors or enters rooms. For another, some of these corridors and offices are already becoming familiar. Now, each time it retraces its steps, the camera must pick on the same small landmarks—the same stain, the same crack, the same notice. The camera must acquire habits just as the inmates of the office have. Again, from now on when the camera looks at windows it must try not to look out of them so that we see the outside world (it can show other *people* looking out of them provided we don't see what they see. This will intensify our desire to look out and therefore get out.) The reiteration and repetition of certain images of stagnation which has already begun—like the Thumb Man, for instance, and Charlie—will help. So will the onset of darkness at the end of the day. Then, as the lights come on in the offices, when you look out all you see is the reflection of your office and yourself. It may even be worth, very gradually, actually lowering the ceilings of the offices and drawing together the walls throughout the film. Only by a foot or so, but the effect might be powerful.

However it is done, claustrophobia must gather in the morning, lift a little at lunch, and regather through the afternoon until by The Departure the office presses upon us to an almost intolerable degree, and people seem not so much to leave the building at the end of the day as to explode from it.

*   *   *

Peter stops in the corridor, wondering who to talk to next. Casting about, he sees Woodrow Bolton apparently approaching the corridor from the stair/lift landing to the left. Apprehensively he darts into the nearest office and shuts the door.

The camera remains on Bolton, who retraces his steps. He seems to be calculating. He now traverses the landing, counting. Every now and then he sniffs.

Jack Ellroyd, the new Vice Chairman and man Bolton is somewhat reluctantly grooming for Chairman, comes up. He is a big man, aged about forty-six, with thick dark hair and a Scarlet Pimpernel forehead. His eyes have a habit of locking on to the person

46

he is talking to, or object being talked about. He has large, over-
(or under-) confident movements.

—ELLROYD: Woodrow. We must have ten minutes together.
We must get this buttoned up.

—BOLTON: Yes, yes. Yes, yes. Didn't Sheila fix you up? I'm
busy at the moment.

—ELLROYD: We've got to have belt and braces.

—BOLTON: I know. Of course. Do you notice anything (pause)
odd? Hmm? Here.

Ellroyd unfixes his eyes and looks around the landing by the
lifts, then over to the stair well. He sees nothing. He finds Bolton
unpredictable. He decides it is an appeal from one disciplinarian
to another.

—ELLROYD: You mean the dirt?

—BOLTON: No, no. You're like an Assistant Adjutant. No. (He
sniffs twice quickly). I may be wrong. Give me ten minutes. I'll be
in my office in ten minutes.

He turns abruptly and walks past the lift to a door marked Fire
Escape. Ellroyd watches him push through it. With an effort he
regains confidence, steps purposefully backwards, turns briskly,
and nearly collides with Cyril.

—CYRIL: Oops. I say. Sorry. Sorry, sir. I've—one moment—
sorry—dislodged a paper I think—ah . . .

He bends to pick it up.

—ELLROYD: What do you do?

—CYRIL (fighting with his bull-dog clip): Wells, sir. Cyril
Wells. In you go. I've been with the firm nine years.

—ELLROYD: I don't want to know who you are. What do you
do?

—CYRIL: I'm in a Progress Section, sir. Checking. Taking
things round. Making sure memos and documents are in plastic
bags. A Progress man, sir.

—ELLROYD: A sort of glorified messenger?

—CYRIL: No, sir. That is, yes, sir. Yes.

—ELLROYD: Do you know Ritson, the Sales Manager for B
Division?

—CYRIL: No, sir. That is—no, I can't say I do, sir.

—ELLROYD: Find him. I think he's in the Old Office somewhere. He's been rung five times this morning. I want a memo he
sent me three weeks ago on Reps' Commissions. Get it for me.

—CYRIL (scribbling on one of his bits of paper): Three weeks

ago. Reps' Commissions. Certainly, sir. Ritson. Right away, sir.
—ELLROYD: Not 'right-a-way'. I want it tomorrow morning.
Give it to my secretary.
—CYRIL: Certainly, sir. To . . .? For . . .? Sir . . .?
—ELLROYD: The Vice Chairman. Ellroyd.

*　　*　　*

Cut to Mr. Bolton. He is half-way up the fire-escape in one of
those deep wells which appear in large buildings either, one sup-
poses, through architectural error or in the mistaken belief that
they let light into the windows that open on to them. We know
the sky, that little tent of blue, is above us. The camera ignores it.
Mr. Bolton is puffing a bit. He continues to climb steadily, looking through nearly all windows, sniffing. (He might be looking
through the windows in the Old Office, which would lead to
the . . .)

*　　*　　*

. . . cut to Ritson. He runs untidily up some narrow wooden
stairs, breaking of more patches of rotten linoleum, and
into his office. This is dusty, crowded, ramshackle. Two heaped
desks are pressed close, face to face, under one small, high-up
window. One old peeling filing cabinet, a screwed up mackintosh
on the floor, a wooden cupboard bursting with paper, full ash-
trays, sagging wire baskets, small electric fire, single hanging
bulb, calendar on the wall, etc.
At the far desk sits Martin. He is twenty-four, small, rather
delicate, with a short, neat beard. He has a pale face.
—RITSON (mild panic): Have any of the buggers rung again?
What do they want, for Christ's sake? You told them I was seeing
the South London Reps.
—MARTIN: Yes.
—RITSON: That gives us a moment to prepare defensive positions. Get out the Reps' files. Give me the sales reports and order
records. You say Ellroyd's secretary rang?
—MARTIN: Five times. She rang again after I'd said you were
seeing the South London Reps.
—RITSON: I've seen this coming.
He belches. A pause while he scans the sales reports and order

48

records. He lights a cigarette. His fingers are nicotine stained, but strong and well-shaped, the nails well kept.

—RITSON: God, these sales figures are terrible. Terrible. I wonder if we could cook the books. We'll have to.

—MARTIN: Won't they find out? They're bound to in the end.

—RITSON: A good Sales Manager always cooks the books. I don't mean dishonesty. It's like the Governor of the Bank of England keeping up foreign confidence with false gold reserves. I keep up the confidence of the Directors and Chairmen—in this case the Vice Chairman.

—MARTIN: And if they improve?

—RITSON: Then you level down again. It's a bit complicated. You often have to take from one Rep and give to another—so long as they get the right commission and that the quarterly results are correct. I'll show you how to do it. Pick out all the Reps with very erratic results. Very good and very bad. Those are the ones to work with.

They work in silence for a while, Martin going through files, Ritson making notes and calculations. They continue working during the following conversation.

—RITSON: God, I feel randy this morning. I feel so randy I could have a horse. It's these bloody hangovers. You know what they say—'Catch a man with a hangover . . .' I can't remember how it goes on. Do you ever feel like that?

—MARTIN: Often. But I'm far too frightened to do anything about it. Frightened of Anne for one thing. (Pause.) Do you ever feel guilty about Angela?

—RITSON: Of course. Drunken guilt. Sober guilt. I love her, you know—but eighteen years is a long time. I love the children. She knows that. Have you ever noticed that loving children and sex go together? Liking sex and liking children, I mean. It's true—but, oh, I suddenly thought years ago—what a pity to waste all that lovely lust on just Angela. (Pause.) It's also something to do with being Catholic . . .

Pause, while they work.

—RITSON (impelled): I'll have to do something about it. My balls are boiling. Let's see——

He goes through a rather worn address book, thumbed, pencilled entries.

—RITSON (dubious): Um . . .

He picks up the telephone.

—RITSON: Give me a line please.

He dials. Pause.

—RITSON: Deidre? Hullo, darling, it's Geoffrey. (Pause.) How are you? (Pause.) Oh, I'm sorry, what is it? Anything special? (Pause.) Well, how about coming out to lunch. (Pause.) Oh, why, dear? (Pause.) Why? (Pause.) I'm sorry. I—— (Pause.) Please, Deidre, we could go to the Regina. (Pause.) I didn't ... (Pause.) Oh—— (Pause.) Look, just lunch, Deidre. I promise ... (Pause.) Deidre ... Deidre ...

She cuts him off. Ritson replaces the receiver, his eyebrows raised. He rapidly (instantly) regains his composure.

—RITSON: She's neurotic as hell. Thinks she hates sex and says she's a lesbian. The lot. She's no more lesbian than my arsehole. Actually, what it is is she hates *liking* sex—you know? It makes her wild in bed.

—MARTIN: Not exactly. (Pause.) When you say 'wild in bed'— tell me, what exactly do you *do*, Geoffrey?

—RITSON (flipping through his book again): How do you mean? Fucking? Oh, nothing special. Sometimes ...

The phone rings. He picks it up.

—RITSON: Hullo, Ritson. (Pause.) Harry! How are you! (Pause.) Fine. Listen, Harry. I was going to ring you. I've a big call to make, then I'll ring you back. We've got some fiddling to do. Ellroyd on the rampage. (Pause.) Yes. I'll tell you. (Pause.) 'Bye.

He replaces the receiver and immediately picks it up again and dials another number. A pause.

—RITSON: Hullo—is your mother in? (Pause.) It's Geoff here. Hullo love. (Pause.) Look can you make the Regina Palace at One o'clock? (Pause.) One thirty? (Pause.) OK—see you.

He replaces the receiver and at once becomes absorbed in his work. He whistles. Martin looks at him enigmatically. Ritson reaches in front of him for a cigarette.

        *   *   *

Cut to close-up of two cigarettes hovering over an ashtray. They are quivering, incessantly tapped.

Pull back to show Janice and her new friend Diane gossiping fiercely.

Diane works at a small 'spur' switchboard—that is to say by herself, in charge of about thirty-eight or so extensions which for some reason are not yet connected to the main system. The camera is observing them both from the far side of a glass door, so that although we are quite close and can see every detail of their expression and observe the rather old-fashioned blinking metal eyelids of the switchboard (one of which is active at the start of the conversation), we can hear nothing.

Diane is squat and thickset. She has a square, dark face with a massive ridge of eyebrow straight across the middle, a pug nose and a ludicrously large mouth, far larger and sloppier than Janice's, with a great many small twisted teeth. On her chin is a mole the size of a currant, with other smaller ones scattered about. She is dressed in a loose red cardigan, too big for her, and a tight, dirty, short check skirt, too small for her muscular thighs. Her face is immensely expressive. She shoots her eyebrows—eyebrow rather—up and down, she grips Janice's arm, she screams with laughter. They both giggle helplessly, their cigarettes waving, dropping ash. Now fifteen metal eyelids are blinking mechanically, continually, desperately—and uselessly.

We cut to . . .

*   *   *

. . . a Gentlemen's. Lawrence, standing at the urinal, reaches in front of himself. He pees standing tensely to attention. The cistern operates and flushes. Lawrence remains at attention.

He washes his hands. Suddenly, he grips the taps fiercely, bending slightly forward. It is as though he were about to tear the basin out by its roots.

He goes out of the door and we see that the lavatory is obliquely opposite the office of the Thumb Man, whose door is surprisingly ajar. The camera holds on a fairly long shot of the Thumb Man sitting motionless at his desk, while Lawrence walks off screen to return to his office.

People pass and repass. 'Give a lit-ill whis-ill.' Still we watch the Thumb Man. Woodrow Bolton passes. The camera follows him.

*   *   *

Cut to Bolton hurrying into his office. Jack Ellroyd is sitting reading a magazine.

—BOLTON (panting): Sorry to keep you waiting.

—ELLROYD: Been chasing a secretary? Ha ha ha!

—BOLTON: Um.

—ELLROYD: I only want one crack of the whip, Woodrow. It's a question of belt and braces again. *Receuiller pour mieux advancer.* Here are some of the problems. Over half the staff are over fifty. I've had a talk with the Management Consultancy again. Their Time man has rooted out the disturbing fact that our lifts travel 30,000 miles a year. In an office our size they should travel about 15,000. That's two bites at the cherry and no mistake. No wonder our electricity bills are what they are. Reps' commissions need looking into. I've made it mandatory to put all important documents and memos into plastic bags ...

—BOLTON (who has been listening with mounting impatience): Plastic bags! Plastic bags!

—ELLROYD (shrewdly): You'd be surprised how much money is wasted on retyping dirty memos and letters, etc., with thumb marks and so on.

—BOLTON: Jack—leave that sort of thing to Harmer—it's Managing Director stuff. It's not even that—Section Heads, for heaven's sake. What? You're Vice Chairman now, Jack. You'll be Chairman soon. You'll be over, what is it, 3,000 people? Think big. Think very big. Takeovers. Mergers. Diversifying. What about Eastern Europe? I said we must move on that quickly. That's the next big market. When are we going to take some decisions on that?

—ELLROYD: Cameron's arranged a Board meeting for this afternoon.

—BOLTON: Yes and a bloody silly time too. I said to someone no-one will be sober. I *certainly* shan't be sober, you can be sure of that.

—ELLROYD: But, Woodrow, it's your own philosophy. 'Look after the small things and the big things will look after themselves.'

—BOLTON: Ah—you mean the concept of Boss as Enemy? Very sound American Business Theory. At least I think it's American. I may have invented it myself. Once you've built up your firm, your organisation, delegated and so on, then it runs itself. This firm has run itself for fifteen years. The Boss is a

52

galvaniser, a terrifier. He turns up unexpectedly. He strikes where least expected. He spends his time in an apparently maverick way challenging quite sound business principles, just to keep people on their toes. See what I mean? It helps if he drinks a bit. *Then* details are important, but significant details. For example, have you noticed the smell of onions round here the last four days?

—ELLROYD: No.

—BOLTON (narrowed eyes): You don't think that important? You may be right. *May* be. Or take this—a bit of information I picked up this morning—Lawrence Gurney or Burney, a Packaging and Design Group Head, don't suppose you've ever heard of him, can't say I had, but he's ambitious. A roaring, fighting, tough, kick-em-where-it-hurts, ambitious kookie. Could be useful. Do you see what I mean? *That*'s what I call *significant* detail —maverick detail. Not plastic bags.

Pause. He looks enquiringly at Ellroyd. Ellroyd can think of nothing to say.

—BOLTON (magnanimously): Look, forgive me, Jack. It's difficult to delegate after twenty years at the top. You go ahead. You do the job your way. Don't let me interfere. Now, I must rush. I've got some work to do. It may be nothing. But I may be on to something big. Something very big indeed.

*   *   *

Bolton hurries out. We follow him (taking in the ceiling, the descending ceiling) to the lift. He presses the Up button and then stands impatiently tapping his foot. The lift arrives. Inside, Charlie.

—BOLTON: Morning, Charlie. Tenth floor. How's it going?

—CHARLIE: Pretty busy, sir, pretty busy. I've been kept up and down.

—BOLTON: That's the way.

He can think of nothing else to say. This makes him uneasy. He hums. Charlie is completely passive. At the tenth floor Bolton gets out.

—BOLTON: Thanks, Charlie.

Expressionless, Charlie presses all the buttons to the Mezzanine floor. The lift starts to go down, floor by floor. At the seventh, Janice gets in, looks at the buttons all glowing (they are those flat panels of glass, not buttons really, which glow when you touch them), then looks at Charlie.

—JANICE: How you doing, Charlie?

—CHARLIE: Some joker pressed all the buttons. I'm late for my tea as it is.

—JANICE: Did they really? Isn't that a shame.

They stop at the third floor. Janice gets out.

—JANICE: Thanks, Charlie.

Charlie appears quite indifferent to her flighty bottom, her almost bouncing breasts. He continues his stopping journey to the Mezzanine floor where he will have a silent tea with one of the packers. The camera follows Janice, swinging, bouncing, glancing —along the corridor and into her office. Peter it talking to Lawrence.

—PETER: ... and *apparently*, my dear, the first sentence was 'My hot plates satisfy my needs.' From Bee! I heard that Jack Ellroyd—I imagine not a fastidious man—when he read it said to his secretary ...

—LAWRENCE (who has been listening with a strained look of interest, a wide, false smile): Could—would you mind if I just interrupted, Peter? Janice, will you take that list into Bob, please. I've put it on your typewriter. And has that letter come yet? Is there a letter for me in the In Tray?

Janice gets up and goes slowly through the In Tray. Shrugs.

—JANICE: No.

—LAWRENCE (resuming his expression): You were saying, Peter ...?

—PETER (feeling that an uninterested audience is better than none): Apparently coarse Jack Ellroyd said to his secretary ...

But the camera follows Janice out, the door closes behind us, and we enter ...

*   *   *

... the Design and Packaging studio. Janice goes up to Bob Glenny's desk and gives him the list. Pause while he slowly reads it. He reads it again.

—BOB: This'll have to wait till after lunch, Janice. I won't have time before. I've an important visit to make at lunch.

He reaches down and, with an effort, pulls up the blue canvas bag, putting it with a thump in front of him.

54

—BOB : Tell Lawrence I'll check the particulars after lunch. I've got to see to this first.

—JANICE : What you got in there then, Bob?

Bob unzips his bag, reaches into it and produces a lump of rock and mud the size of a small turnip.

—BOB : Feel that.

Janice takes it. Her hand drops.

—JANICE : It's heavy. What is it?

—BOB (placidly, impressively): Gold

—JANICE (impressed): Go on! *Gold?*

—BOB : Well, I won't swear to it. But I've been after gold for some time now and I'd say that's gold. I'm getting it analysed during the lunch hour. They can tell you quite quickly.

—JANICE (weighing the gold): But how'd you know? Have you found it before?

—BOB : Oh yes. Yes. Oh yes.

—JANICE : You never have. When, then?

—BOB : First time was about eight years ago.

He looks at his watch, then settles himself.

—BOB : Well, if you're interested, I'll tell you. It all started eight years ago when we were on holiday in Wales. Dolgethly. Well, Dad and I did there just as we do at home. Every evening we'd take the car out for a bit of a spin and then have a pint on the way back. Sometimes we'd stop and have a bit of a walk. You've always got to give a car a bit of a drive every day. It keeps the oil moving and gets it warmed up. Well, we were taking this walk when we found a place where there'd been a fall of rock, and running across it about five feet above the ground, were these thin streaks, thin yellow streaks or veins, right across. My dad said—'I think that's gold, Bob.' Well, we were quite excited. We didn't expect much, but we managed to get out some pieces, some chunks and put them in the boot. We brought them back and I brought them up to London and took them to the Geological Museum in Kensington and asked their opinion. Sure enough— they said it was gold.

—JANICE : No!

—BOB : Not too pure. A lot of dirt—what they call paydirt. But real gold. Well, naturally enough Dad and I were pretty excited. I took the next Friday off and we drove up to Dolgethly that weekend. We took two spades and a pick.

—JANICE : What happened?

55

—BOB : Do you know, we couldn't find it! We found the area all right, but there's been mining in that area and there's quite a lot of subsidence. Where we thought it was was all tumbled about with quite recent disturbance.

—JANICE : Oh, what a pity. What a pity you hadn't really loaded up. You might have been rich. Just think of it.

—BOB : Well, naturally we were a bit disappointed. But that put us on the track. After that we went prospecting every holiday. Often we'd get as far as Dolgethly or Barmouth for a weekend.

—JANICE : Did you ever find any more?

—BOB (easily, filling and lighting his pipe) : You'd be surprised how much gold there is in England. We used to export gold, you know. If you're interested——

He opens a drawer and pulls out a map. Janice leans over his shoulder.

—BOB : The experts will tell you that the main centres are Wales and Scotland—and for quite a time I believed them. We used to go picking about in the old workings—here and here, and here for instance (pipe jabs)—and you can pick up quite a bit. We did that for a few years, but it's not prospecting. You don't get very much.

Pause. Bob puts his pipe in his mouth and looks at Janice. He takes his pipe out.

—BOB : I began to wonder if the experts were right. I suddenly got the notion that there was probably a good deal more gold in England than what they knew. There's Silsbury Hill—do you know that legend? There was meant to be a solid gold horse buried under this great hill at Silsbury, Wiltshire. Well, no doubt that was taken by tomb robbers—but how was it made? My idea is out of Wiltshire gold. There's silver and jasper and amethyst in Cornwall, and tin. You get a bit of amethyst in Wales, too. Onyx and garnets in Scotland. Marcasite near Folkestone. Then agates —that's Cornwall again. Oh, there's scatterings of wealth all over England for those prepared to look. So recently we've turned our attention to Kent, that's where I live. And almost at once Dad had a big strike in the side of a ditch not eight miles away, but he hasn't been able to find it again. He's eighty now, so of course his memory sometimes fails him, but he's almost as strong as he was.

But now we've made a really big strike. These here are the first specimens. If they're good quality—not too much paydirt—then I think we're on to something. (He winks.)

—JANICE: How much, Bob?

—BOB (shrewdly): £5,000 a year. £7,000 a year. And these are conservative estimates.

The telephone begins to ring. Bob ignores it. He has to finish his paragraph, his train of thought.

—BOB: Dad's working at it now. My eldest boy is helping him. My wife washes the lumps down in the sink—what you might call the ore. I can tell you, it's becoming quite an industry.

He picks up the telephone.

—BOB: Bob Glenny speaking. (Pause.) Yes. (Pause.) OK, Lawrence.

He replaces receiver.

—BOB: Well, you'd better be getting back to Lawrence. He wants you. I've quite enjoyed our little talk, Janice. I ... mmm ...

—JANICE: I'd best be off, then. Let us know if they say it's gold.

—BOB: Yes, I will.

Janice goes to the door. Bob watches her go out, his pipe in his mouth, one hand resting on his gold.

*   *   *

Cut to Janice coming into Lawrence's office.

—LAWRENCE: What on earth have you been doing, Janice? Where have you been?

—JANICE: Talking to Bob. He may be going to get £7,000 a year.

—LAWRENCE: You spend more time out of this office than you do in it.

—JANICE (conscious of the effect she has on him, indifferent): Well, there's not much to do here, is there? We're not exactly snowed under, are we?

—LAWRENCE (shouting): What the bloody hell do you ...

He stops himself. He bows his head forward, hands clenched to his temples. He masters himself.

—LAWRENCE: I'm sorry. I'm in a bit of a state today. I didn't mean that.

—JANICE (shrugging): Please yourself.

—LAWRENCE: Go and see if Chris is still with Peter, will you? I want a word with him.

*

Like Lawrence's eyes, the camera follows Janice's legs out into the corridor. The corridor is full of moving legs. The camera is suddenly caught, as it were, by another pair and carried back along the corridor. To be caught again and carried forward. Back and forward, eddying for a moment below a notice board. Then it seems about to make real progress. A sturdy pair of female legs carry it up the stairs, half-way along the corridor and start down the fourth floor.

But now its attention is taken by two short, thin legs which carry it back. These legs, though short and almost spindly, take enormous, slow strides. They imitate much longer, more secure legs. They bounce at the toes—huge steps with a quick, nervous bounce at the end. They are nervous legs trying to seem solid, and they reveal this at the stairs when they suddenly blur into a very rapid, millipede descent.

They continue their ponderous, jerky goosestep until they reach a door. They stop. Bounce. There is the sound of a knock, the door opens, and the legs, bridging an enormous gulf, step in.

*

The camera pulls back to show Cyril Wells in Bee's office. Bee, without shame, is removing all her make-up with a large wodge of cotton wool covered in cold cream. This is held in her right hand, in her left a hand-mirror. Stripped of make-up her face has an early morning look, the texture of the skin reptilian.

—BEE (screwing up her face, cleaning it with a wodge of cotton wool): Yes?

—CYRIL: Awfully sorry to barge in like this, Bee. I meant to last time, but overlooked it, so I thought I'd just pop in now to warn you, though you got the memo we established.

—BEE: What are you talking about?

—CYRIL (searching swiftly through his papers): No. No. No. Where's it gone? I had it only—ah!—no. *Yes*. Some time after lunch. They'll only take a few minutes. If you could just let the men in to take out your desk and bring in the new one.

—BEE (her right hand, gripping the cotton wool, ominously still): What was that?

—CYRIL: Yes, I'm afraid it will mean emptying the drawers. But they'll have the desk out in no time. And the new one in.

—BEE (quietly): I'm sorry, Cyril. No desk is going out of this room. I do not intend to lose my desk at this stage of my life.

—CYRIL (nervously uncomprehending): Oh, ha ha ha ha ha. Oh, that's a good one, Bee. Oh dear. Wait till I tell Jessie. One of your best. Oh, ha ha ha. (He backs agitatedly away, wiping his eyes.) Well—I'd best—oh dear—be . . .

—BEE (rising to her feet): No bloody desk is coming into this office. That's flat. I shall not change my desk.

—CYRIL: Oh, Bee—well, I am sorry—but it's nothing to do with me. You had the memo.

—BEE: What memo? I've had no memo. Nothing at all. No warning. No consultation.

—CYRIL (shuffling through his papers): Oh, I thought we'd established . . . Oh God . . . Well, in that case I bear some measure, I could be said, at second-hand, to responsibility . . .

—BEE: Well, if you're responsible, just get this clear Cyril. I've been here some years now. I think I can say without undue modesty, well, I have established a certain position. And I will not, repeat not, *tolerate* having myself and my desk and my office moved about from pillar to post. Is that clear? I will not *tolerate* it.

She raises up the wodge of cotton wool and with a 'magnificent gesture' hurls it to the carpet beside one of the waste-paper baskets.

—CYRIL (backing away): Point taken. Point taken. But it's nothing to do with me, Bee. It really isn't. I *may* be—the *memo*, possibly. I let it go astray. But the desk is—no—nothing to do with me. Nothing. The Office Manager, Mr. Braine. Mr. Braine. Yes —Mr. Braine.

—BEE: Mr. Braine.

She sits down and picks up the telephone and buff-coloured office telephone list. Cyril runs from the room. Bee dials, listens.

—BEE: Mr. Braine! It's Bee Dugdale here. There's been some trivial mistake. I wonder if you could sort it out? They're trying to take my desk. Well, naturally I've no intention of letting *that* happen. I wonder if you would just sort it out? (Pause.) What?

59

(Pause.) Well, that may be—I had no warning or consultation—but that's not the point. I'm afraid I will not have my desk moved, so please arrange that it is not moved. (Pause.) You have? (Pause.) Look, Mr. Braine. I have been in this firm a good many years now. I'm afraid I cannot allow myself just to be pushed about like so much flotsam you know. I don't want a new desk and I will not have a new desk. Is that . . .?

* * *

Cut to Cyril Wells' office. He is sitting at his desk, distractedly shuffling his papers, his forehead wrinkling and unwrinkling. At the other desk sits Jessie, aged about sixty, a grey bun low on her head, spectacles attached by a loop of black ribbon round her thin neck, an impression of lace.

—CYRIL: I don't know how much more I can take. I told her I wasn't responsible. I wish I could find that memo record. Ranting and shouting at me. I explained that Mr. Braine was the man she needed.

—JESSIE: Quite the Queen Bee and all her merry staff, were we?

—CYRIL: I've never known her so bad.

—JESSIE: Well, we have our little temper. Temper temper, now, temper temper.

—CYRIL: Yes. Now. (Pause.) Let me look—um—Jessie, I'll need four hundred plastic bags this afternoon.

—JESSIE: Of course the first of our weapons is the plastic bag. A big job on, have we?

Cyril and Jessie's office is physically next door to Bee's, though to get from one to the other a circular walk is necessary. Now a loud, muffled thump comes through the wall.

—CYRIL (involuntary spasm): God!

—JESSIE: Our Lord and Master up to her little tricks again.

* * *

Cut to Bee still on the telephone. She is speaking in a low, fierce voice:

—BEE: I am sorry it has come to this Mr. Braine. I am afraid you leave me with no alternative but to speak to the Chairman. I have, as you know, a certain position in this firm. I do not think

60

Bolly will see the matter your way. In fact I'm sure he won't. In fact I am very glad indeed I am not in your shoes at this moment, Mr. Braine. Goodbye.

She replaces the receiver with a short, vicious jab. She is trembling. In an effort to retain control she continues to cleanse her face, using rather too much cream. Involuntary explanations and isolated words are forced out of her as she considers the enormity of this attempt on her position. Though still seething she eventually appears to have mastered herself again. She picks up the telephone and dials deliberately.

—BEE: Oh, Sheila. Bee here. Could I have a word with Bolly? (Pause.) What? (Pause.) Well, where is he? Can you find him, please? This is very urgent. I must speak to him. (Pause.) What? (Pause.) Could you please find him . . .?

Suddenly she starts shouting. She bangs her hand, still holding the cream-covered cotton wool, on to her desk. Blobs and smears of cream appear on the desk.

—BEE (shouting): WELL WHERE IS HE? WHERE IS HE? HE'S CHAIRMAN OF THIS COMPANY. I DEMAND TO SPEAK TO HIM. WHERE THE BLOODY HELL IS HE?

*   *   *

Cut to blackness. Echoing sounds of large water cisterns filling and emptying, the rumblings of lift workings. Our eyes become accustomed to the darkness. We see that we are somewhere in the vast attic of the office block. We appear to have crawled into the narrow space beneath a large brick tank. The space is only a foot high but seems, because of the darkness, to stretch infinitely all round. Actually the tank divides the huge roof area in half, and the gap beneath it is due to some mismeasurement or eccentricity of construction.

The camera is inching forward. Despite the almost total darkness we can just see that someone is beside us, inching forward on their stomach. Sound of heavy breathing.

It is Mr. Bolton. He is somewhat dishevelled, but looks determined and excited. Every now and then he stops to get his breath. He breathes deeply, sniffs.

Suddenly a dim light appears ahead. He is nearly through to the second half of the roof area. The space ahead becomes even lower. Mr. Bolton hurries.

61

Now we can see into the new roof area. It contains tanks, pipes, dusty, empty stretches with lift workings like small mine shafts rising out of them. Some broken chairs and empty cans. And across the foreground a large, square extractor shaft for ventilation. It comes across from the right and goes straight out at the left, presumably to the open air where it will discharge its fumes. The extractor fans are working, because the shaft has a few holes and rents in it and we can see cobwebs and dust blowing around these.

Mr. Bolton eyes this with excitement. He sniffs deeply, then, kicking out, struggles towards it.

After a few inches it is evident he is sticking. The gap is too narrow. Mr. Bolton begins to fight powerfully, almost wildly. He thrashes with his feet and claws with his hands. After a few minutes the effort is too much and he has to stop, his head collapsed, eyes shut, panting.

The cobwebs move. The extractor continues to extract, thrusting towards Mr. Bolton its mixture of odours.

His eyes open. He sets his jaw, narrows his eyes, and, in a final supreme effort, goes into what seems some form of convulsion. He hammers his legs and knees and arms furiously against the ten-inch apart floor and ceiling, veins bulge and throb, he heaves and thrusts, by a miracle moves an inch or two, surely lifting the giant tank on his shoulders, then sticks again, and again strains and pulls and kicks.

Suddenly he collapses, gasping and panting, sweat pouring down his face.

After a few minutes he revives. This time, admitting defeat, he wearily raises his hands to push himself back.

He doesn't move. He pushes harder. Still no movement. Flexing his shoulders he pushes with sustained force. He is stuck.

The same fury, less forceful through exhaustion, is now employed to extricate him from the very position it has placed him in. Banging at the concrete four inches above his heels, he tries to twist himself round. He sweeps and rasps his hands in circular movements across the floor under his nose.

Once more he collapses, once more revives.

—MR. BOLTON (hoarsely panting, but loud): Help! Help! Help! Help!

His head falls on his hands. He looks up again, struggles feebly. Stops.

62

—MR. BOLTON: I'm stuck! Help me! Help! Help! I'm stuck! Help!

* * *

The camera pulls back from Mr. Bolton. Slowly at first—he becomes invisible in the darkness, his cries faint—then faster and faster, skimming back over the cluttered roof area. Abruptly it stops, and then plunges down to the floor.

But here it does not stop. It plunges straight through the floor. There is a blur of close-up brick, darkness, steel ribs and concrete bones, wires, pipes, rods—intestines. We are passing through the actual body of the office.

This is the penultimate addition to the morning's claustrophobia which, starting when the camera ceased to look out of the windows and took in the ceilings and the floor (the leg sequence), intensified with Mr. Bolton, and now culminates in . . .

* * *

. . . the Thumb Man. We are in his office, looking down upon the back of his large, almost bald head. The sound of the Vent-Axia. The light, of course, is on to supplement, or rather to perform the function of, the inadequately lighting skylight.

He is looking at his thumb. We close slowly on this until its ridges fill the screen.

We must hold this close-up for four minutes. Not as a still, but exploring with minute movements, going in a little closer, then moving a little further away, moving round a fraction so that we can see the hump of the nail. Possibly the thumb itself moves a millimetre once or twice.

Its ridges fill the screen. They are like the map contours of an extremely steep mountain, or a diagram of a complex irrigation system. The thumb is an almost microscopic close-up of an aphis grub, a segment of corduroy trouser. It resembles the strata at a cliff face, those lines where the congealing rock has been thrust upwards and sideways and then frozen. We begin to see, so diverting and varied is it, why he looks at it all the time; life in the grain of a thumb. Then, so gradually it is impossible to say when it started, minute molecules of moisture begin to gather in the thumb—a mist condensing on the mountain, dew forming in the

63

irrigation system. The aphis is secreting, secretes until a large drop is formed and runs down one of the runnels. The thumb is weeping.

We cut abruptly to the Thumb Man walking downstairs. Cut to him going into the lift. Cut to him coming out, past Charlie still sitting in his chair. Cut to him out in the street.

The camera pulls back and up. Up and up and up, soaring above the street, the cars, the office, until it is as high as it was at the beginning when we watched Bolton's car coming across Waterloo Bridge and watched the patterns of streaming people converging on their work.

LUNCH

FAR below, two figures are walking slowly on a roof. They are in the centre of the screen. The camera zooms in and closes on them.

It is Lawrence and Chris. Lawrence is eating a sandwich in his left hand, holding a plastic box containing three others in his right hand. Chris has a large cold cheap pie.

—LAWRENCE: I used to come up here and have a sandwich when I first joined. As I said, I did a year here, then eight in Manchester. Now I've been here just over seven.

He suddenly stops and looks at Chris. A friendly look.

—LAWRENCE: Look, Chris—why don't you get out?

—CHRIS (a little embarrassed): But I don't want to. Of course I get a bit depressed at times—but I quite like it. Isn't it a good job?

—LAWRENCE: It depends what you mean by good.

—CHRIS: But I thought you liked it. You've always seemed to till this morning. I know . . .

He looks down, now definitely embarrassed, out of his depth. He would like to say 'I know you're having a bad time with your wife. Are you sure it isn't that?'

—CHRIS: Well, I know how difficult things can get. Piling up . . .

—LAWRENCE (quizzical, amused): I hate it. I started off hating it. No—that's not quite true. Actually the only times I can remember when I was excited or ambitious were up here.

They have reached the front of the building, the prow. Dark clouds are coming up from the horizon, the wind getting stronger, but the sun is still shining. Ahead and around them roofscape, other giant office blocks.

—LAWRENCE (gesturing around): You see how like ships they are? Look at those flags there in the wind. I used to imagine this building setting off like a great liner, grinding everything in its path to dust, smashing its way through towards those clouds, and then out to sea with me on the bridge.

But that was more—what? A sort of visual fantasy. Something

E   65

more because of them looking like ships than actually wanting to be a captain of industry. Even then I hated it, in fact particularly then. I can remember sitting in my horrid little office and having to go to the bog to cry, literally cry. I think that was mostly a physical reaction. Instinctive. I mean how can you expect someone of twenty-three, just down from Reading University— well in fact I was just back from France, even worse—how can you expect them to spend the whole time, all day, shut up in a box? It's quite fiendish, like a zoo. For twenty-three years I had been— compared to *that*—free. School, holidays, National Service, Reading—I *was* free. And then suddenly they shut you up for eight hours every day. Eight hours in a small box. No wonder I cried. And it's far worse than prison. It's not a punishment—it's your reward! This eight by ten box is your reward for passing exams, doing what you were told, trying hard to please. Your reward is to sit in that box for the rest of your life.

—CHRIS (defensively, even a little aggressively, feeling himself threatened, reacting to the note in Lawrence's voice): Well, why didn't you leave, Lawrence, if you hated it so much?

—LAWRENCE (only just listening, his obsession beginning to overwhelm him): Why didn't I leave? I know. I've wondered that. It's quite complicated, isn't it? Fear, at bottom I suppose. Of course, they train you to obey from the pot upwards. They say it's better to keep your first job for two or three years otherwise you get the reputation of a non-stayer. Then you've got to get a commercial training. (For Christ's sake what had I been doing for twenty-three years but training? They should have used *that* time better.) Well, then I got married and we went to Manchester and Helen had a baby. We didn't know anyone in Manchester. That made things frightening. I felt I only had Helen and my job between me and—what? I don't know. Total nakedness—loneliness. Destitution. Annihilation. And of course we needed money. For some reason I thought if I left I'd never get another job. *Ever*. Ridiculous fears—but once you give way to them . . .

Then we did make a few friends. Not a lot—Helen's never been very good at making friends. But somehow knowing them and keeping the job seemed connected. If I left the job I'd lose the friends. And of course it kept getting nearer the time we'd be leaving Manchester. It didn't seem worth it when there was only a couple of years.

Pause.

—LAWRENCE: And it does something physical to you, you know. I don't just mean habit, though God knows what channels it must have gouged in my brain. But when I hated it, when I really hated—after a weekend or a holiday or some humiliation or just realising I was trapped suddenly—I used to feel my head was exploding. I used to feel on fire. I think thousands of my brain cells were being literally destroyed. It's a sort of shock treatment. They break down, physically kill your centres of resistance. Gradually the attacks get less, your capacity to hate gets less. You see them here in this office, men over fifty, their faces are washed out, brain-washed, going about their drivelling tasks, they're just zombies.

Pause.

—LAWRENCE (thinking aloud): Except they don't entirely stop. Every now and again you burst. You decide to leave. Look at some situation ads. But that's destructive too. 'Letting off steam.' Letting it escape. Not letting it build up so that it really blows you up. A safety device, another trap.

Pause.

—LAWRENCE (thinking aloud): My head got cluttered up. Bits of plastic, cardboard, paper. It stops you thinking. I couldn't think. You know, when we go on holiday the first six or seven days I feel I'm standing on my head and it's all coming out. The great clattering, cluttering pile of rubble, of slogans, memos, instructions, boxes, pouring out of my mouth. And then, just when I'm free of it all, when I'm clean—back we have to go. Back into the shit.

Long pause. Lawrence starts to walk slowly again. Chris walking beside him, head down. The clouds are beginning to obscure the sun.

—LAWRENCE (thinking aloud): And of course there's hope. I want to write you know. I thought a fairly undemanding job would let me write at home, that I'd have a best-seller or something and escape. Football pools. I suppose everyone hopes— actually expects—money will just pour down the chimney one day. A million pounds all over the living-room floor. You just expect not to be at work next week. Something will have happened.

And time passes. You're too young to know about time passing. I don't mean to be patronising, but it's true. It's not till quite a lot of time has passed that it actually becomes visible, if you know what I mean. Helen had another child and then another. We've

67

got three. You have to pay the mortgage on a house. And because it's so easy you get more frightened. I learnt all there is to know about Packaging and Design in two months. What I have to do in a day I could do in twenty minutes. A week's work in an hour and a half say. That's another physical thing—trivial, pointless work. Doing trivial work grinds away your brain. You destroy it. I've been terrified for years that I can't do anything else now. And so you start to hide it, hide everything. I was wrong when I said you lose your hate. Your hate becomes so great you can't face it. It grows and grows and spreads all through you. You start to do terrible things to people you love, to your wife, your children.

They are at the edge of the roof, looking over the parapet to the street eleven floors below.

—LAWRENCE: I've had some bad moments when I've seen what's happening. You can only face it for moments. This last year has been the worst. You probably thought how enthusiastic I was, how keen. I've had to whip it up, get up a great lather of enthusiasm to blot out what I was feeling, to keep going at all. And I *wanted* a life. I wanted things. I've done nothing. Nothing at all.

Swamped, he stares down into the street.

—LAWRENCE: I suppose that sounds like self-pity. But I hate them. Oh God, how I hate them. And I hate myself. I don't know which I hate most; them for doing it to me, or me for letting them do it. Quite honestly, I think I know what Samson felt. If I knew they'd come too, I'd like to fling myself down there. I'd jump right now if I knew it would smash them, break them, destroy them. Destroy them.

Long pause. Grey clouds have come right up over the sky. A wind is blowing, blowing Lawrence's long, thinning hair over his face. Chris stares down, fixes his eyes on a bus creeping along below, trying to think of something to say. At last—

—CHRIS: Why . . . what made you . . . how, *now* . . .?

—LAWRENCE (quickly): You mean why did I suddenly tell you all this? Or do you mean how can I stand staying here if I feel like this? I was coming to that. In fact I can't think why I've got so worked up. That's the wonderful thing—I'm leaving! I've taken the step at last. I'm going. I'm giving up my job. I'm resigning.

Lawrence's mood abruptly reverses. Furious despair, on its head, becomes manic elation. The lines of bitterness double as lines of laughter. He hurries Chris up and down the roof, ob-

68

livious of the rain, gesturing, laughing.

—LAWRENCE: I've got a new job quite near here. Of course I'd
never dare leave without that. And the wonderful thing is that it's
a writing job. Old ambitions never die, they only fade away. Ha
ha ha. Not even that in this case. When I say writing I don't mean
real writing of course. It's a job as a copywriter in an Advertising
Agency. But at least I'll be handling *words*, juggling with words,
living with words. That's the great thing.

—CHRIS: How'd you get it?

—LAWRENCE: A friend who works in the Agency suggested I
try. He knew I wanted a change. I'd never have dared try myself,
just out of the blue, of course. And without another job I'd never
have dared tell you. In fact, I don't think I'd have dared *feel* my
real feelings if it hadn't been for the new job. It was only when I
knew more or less for certain that I'd *got* it that it all welled up. I
suddenly realised how much I'd been hating it here. I realised it
was *that* that was at the bottom of my other difficulties. Mostly
that, anyway. No need to go into them now. But I'm going to lead
an entirely different life, until I'm better. No clutter. No possessions. No people. Just one small, clean, bare room. White walls. A
bed. A table. A chair. During the day I'll learn how to use words.
Hack out advertising copy from words. Then in the evenings I'll
do my own work.

—CHRIS: What'll you write?

—LAWRENCE (sweeping on): I'll go on with what I started
years ago. Did I never tell you? It's an opera—a libretto rather—
about the Bessemer steel process. It may sound a little odd when
you first hear about it, but actually it's a marvellous subject, a
natural. Old Bessemer himself was an extraordinary man, a fascinating life, and then his steel process—it's Wagnerian! Think
of the music! And behind it the roar of the molten steel, blasted
with air. And old Bessemer yelling—singing rather—'More Manganese! More Ferromanganese! More Ferromanganese!' Oh—
great stuff! Great stuff! (He rubs his hands together.) I'd got
quite far with it. It's really quite exciting.

—CHRIS: What made you give it up?

—LAWRENCE: I showed it to an agent about six years ago.
What he said made me give it up. Imagine it. One man! That's
typical of the fear that's kept me here. I should have scoured
London. Anyway, I've sent it to the Advertising Agency. In fact,
that's the point. When I said I'd got the job, I haven't actually

had it confirmed in writing yet. But they told me that was only a formality. The Packaging and Design world and Advertising are very much the same. In fact, most Agencies now have a Packaging department. But I didn't want the same job somewhere else. I've passed their test. They—or rather the Senior Creative Director who was away—just wanted to look at what I'd written to see, as it were, what I'd done creatively. In fact my friend rang up yesterday and said I could make my plans more or less assuming it was in the bag as far as he could gather. He said I'd get the letter this morning. I suppose it will come by the afternoon post. (Pause.) This rain . . . let's go in. Goodness, I'm quite wet.

They go through the roof door and the camera dissolves through after them to . . .

* * *

. . . a small office where three young secretaries—Jill, Christine, Sue (who is Bee Dugdale's secretary)—are having canteen lunch. This a cup of soup, salad, sandwiches, cheese and rolls on a plastic tray. Janice comes in carrying her tray. She smokes while she eats.

—JANICE: I had to take Peter a tray. He said it's the first time he's had a canteen lunch since he's been with the firm. He said (she imitates him), 'It reminds me of the war. Pilchards' heads in tomato sauce.'

—CHRISTINE (sitting by the window): He should try it sometimes. It's not that bad today. It's quite good.

—SUE: Why's he staying in, then? Been stood up?

—JANICE: He says it's going to rain and he's broke.

—SUE: I don't half fancy Peter.

—JANICE: I know. I told him.

—SUE: You never! Oh, Jan—what shall I do? Oh how *embarrassing*! When? What'd he say, then?

—JANICE: He was quite pleased. He said (imitating), 'Does she? Well, that's very nice of her, very nice of her indeed.'

—JILL (sitting by the window, out of which the camera is temporarily allowed to look): I think he's a queer. You can tell.

—JANICE: I wonder.

—SUE: Yes, I don't think he is, either. You can't always tell. Look at the time he spends with Bee.

—JILL: Well, that's queer enough! I don't know how you

stand her, Sue, I really don't. She's so *rude*.

—SUE : You get used to her. She's a bit pathetic really. They're trying to take her desk away. She's mad at them, really mad.

—JANICE : I wondered why she was still sitting there.

—SUE : Yes, she's guarding it. She said they'd probably strike at lunch. I've got to take over when I've had mine.

—JILL : Look, there's Charlie.

The camera closes on her and then passes her, through the window, and focuses on a small figure walking in the street below.

—JILL : He always goes up there, every day. I wonder what he's doing?

—JANICE : He probably has it off with someone in the park.

—JILL (laughs) : He couldn't if he tried. Poor Charlie.

Their voices fade as the camera closes on to Charlie and . . .

        *   *   *   *

. . . follows him up the street.

To indicate that the lunch events do not happen chronologically but overlap, the weather has to alter. For instance, it is still not raining, to show that we are now about a third of the way through Lawrence's speech. Perhaps the same plane could pass overhead. (But there is no need to strain after the simultaneity of events. It does not particularly matter if the effect is not achieved.)

Although in fact the sun is shining, Charlie is wearing a mackintosh. It is too long for him. He also wears a rather high, shapeless hat. He carries a paper carrier bag.

During lunch everyone we see just after they have left the office is in a different street, continuing to impress the size of the office.

Charlie continues slowly up, say, Savoy Street. The camera finally closes on to the back of his mackintosh and dissolves through to another mackintosh being pulled off a filing cabinet.

        *   *   *

It is Ritson. He pulls the mackintosh on and then goes over to a piece of broken mirror propped on a shelf and starts to comb his hair, squinting at his face and pulling it about. Martin tilts back his chair and watches.

71

—RITSON: I need a drink. What's the time? I did book the Regina, didn't I? I think I may have to slip out now and have a quick drink before she gets there. What'll you do?

—MARTIN: Nothing. I've got some sandwiches. I'll sit here and think about you.

—RITSON: Why don't you get someone? We could all go out together.

—MARTIN: I'm far too scared. Anyway, I don't think I want to be an old lecher like you.

—RITSON (pleased, weak smile): Yes. I'm disgusting, aren't I?

Martin smiles, tilting.

—RITSON: Isn't there anyone in the office? They're not bad, some of them.

—MARTIN: There's a girl on the third floor of the New Block I quite fancy.

—RITSON: Go and ask her.

—MARTIN: I don't even know her name. I don't know who she works for. I'm not even sure if it's the third floor. Anyway, she's taller than me.

—RITSON: You don't understand. Ask her. Listen, I'll tell you the whole secret. Girls like fucking. That's all there is to it. I didn't realise that till I was twenty. It's the great breakthrough. Some people never make it. I wish I'd made it earlier. God, when I think of the energy I wasted on handkerchiefs and pillows and —oh, extraordinary things, the rubber handlegrip of a bicycle once, all over the place. But girls and women like fucking as much as men. Most of them. Now you just go up to her and ask her if she'd like to come and have a drink in the pub tonight. She may cheek you, but if she likes the look of you she'll come.

—MARTIN: I might. I feel quite weak with terror at the idea.

—RITSON: And don't worry about size. I had a huge girl in the army once who was six foot three and thin. Long Annie. She worked in the Naafi. She was really nice, like a snake. As I say girls and women . . . God my genitals are churning just to think about it. I think I'll go now, buy a couple of bottles of wine, and start one in the Regina while I wait. But don't forget what I said. It's true.

He goes to the door but turns just before leaving, pauses, then gives Martin his rueful, slightly self-enamoured smile.

Martin, still tilted, stares after him. The camera closes on his face (a wet, small, timid but rather charming mouth), and dissolves through to Janice and the other secretaries.

*　　　*　　　*

They are now really gossiping. The noise, until we sort it out, is like a lot of sparrows or starlings.

—SUE: You should get some of those new stretch stockings from Peter Robinson. They're really marvellous. They don't ladder, however long you wear them.

—JANICE: Yes, they're really great. This is a pair I'm wearing now. They don't half make Lawrence sit up—you should see his eyes.

—JILL: Has he tried it on yet?

—JANICE: He doesn't dare.

—SUE: He would if you encouraged him.

—JANICE: I get mad at a man who doesn't dare. I see him staring and watching. You should see how he looks at me sometimes! Then he'll make a fuss about something else and I know it's because he doesn't dare do anything else. It really gets me.

—JILL: Why don't you ask to change?

—JANICE: It doesn't seem worth it somehow. But I will if it gets worse. Now his wife's left him it's bound to get worse.

—SUE: One office I worked in we had a man in the office across from us who used to show himself. He could see into our toilets.

—CHRISTINE: Why'd she leave him?

—JANICE (answering them in turn): I bet Lawrence'd like to do that. He's a bit batty really. He threw their furniture out the window. Every bit of a nice new suite. Lucky someone wasn't killed.

—SUE: Isn't it odd? You can never tell about people. I don't know him really, but I've always thought he looked so sweet and gentle. I quite fancied him in a way.

—JANICE: Oh, he's sweet and gentle all right. But talk about not knowing people. You know that girl I was telling you about who's just come to work on that switchboard, Diane?

—CHRISTINE: The one with eyebrows and a wart?

—JANICE: It's a mole. But she has this odd smell, you know what I mean . . . She's nice enough, but honestly, you wouldn't

73

think men would see much in her. Anyway, in the end she did go
out with this Indian.

—SUE: Did anything happen?

—JANICE: Shut the window, Christine, the rain's coming in.
Camera closes on rain.

*   *   *

Cut to rain falling against the double-glazed windows of Mr.
Bolton's office. A rather harassed Miss Sturt is on the telephone,
her hand out behind her as though to ward off the rain.

—MISS STURT: ... one minute, the rain's coming in. Hold
on.

She puts down the receiver and goes to close the windows.
Long white Terylene-muslin curtains billow round her. She goes
back to the telephone.

—MISS STURT: No, I'm afraid you *can't* see Mr. Bolton now,
Mrs. Dugdale. He's had a very tiring morning and is spending
lunch resting in the suite. He is seeing no-one at all. (Pause.) I
can't help that. (Pause.) I'm sorry. (Pause.) Yes, you can see him
at five. (Pause.) No. (Pause.) Goodbye.

She puts back the receiver and goes towards the drink
cupboard at the opposite end of the room. From behind her,
through the open door of the Chairman's suite, comes a loud
groan.

—MISS STURT (stopping, calling): Are you all right, Mr. Bolton?

—MR. BOLTON (voice off, loudly): Yes, perfectly all right. Just a
bit bruised. I've been in tighter spots than that. Bring me some
gin. Where's my gin?

—MISS STURT (moving towards the drink cupboard): Coming,
Mr. Bolton. What do you want to eat?

—MR. BOLTON (voice off): nothing.

—MISS STURT: You must have something to eat. What would
you like?

Pause. Silence.

—MISS STURT: Come on now. How about a nice steak?

Pause. Silence.

—MISS STURT: Mr. Bolton?

—MR. BOLTON (voice off): An anchovy sandwich. Where's my
gin?

74

—MISS STURT (with bottle, glass, tonic, etc., methodical):
Coming.

—MR. BOLTON (voice off): Who's that man who knows about
the offices, where they are, who'd know the layout of the roof, the
plans, Floor Manager or something?

—MISS STURT: Office Manager. Mr. Braine.

—MR. BOLTON (voice off): Braine. Get him up here now. At
once. Tell him to bring all his plans and maps. I want to see the
plans of the roof and as many of the adjoining offices as he's got.
Pause.

—MR. BOLTON (voice off. Suddenly suspicious): Why are you
taking so long with my gin? Are you pouring? You're pouring.
I'll do the pouring. Bring the bottle and everything through here,
Sheila. Don't you pour.

Miss Sturt, who has been doing just this, makes a resigned
expression and picks up the bottle to put on a tray.

* * *

Dissolve through to another hand picking up another bottle.

It is Ritson collecting his wine. He puts the second bottle into
the Wine Shop's paper bag and goes out into the street. It is just
beginning to rain.

The camera becomes Ritson, looking at the street through his
eyes. He only sees girls. His eyes fasten onto their lips, their
eyes, their breasts, their legs, their bottoms. If a girl is partly
hidden by the bus stop or another person, he moves his head.
Sometimes a girl catches his eye and looks away, sometimes they
stare back. Sometimes he only pauses on a girl for an instant,
rejecting her; sometimes he follows a girl with his eyes for a long
time, far up the street, until we only just see her, just see her legs,
miss her, see her head again, and lose her. The streets are
thronged, seething with girls. His bus comes. The camera looks
up the skirt of the girl going up the stairs. She has long blonde
hair. The camera follows her and sits next to her. But she is extremely plain, a fact acknowledged by the camera because it
instantly turns and looks out of the window. Girls. The bus starts.
The camera becomes enamoured of some exceptionally pretty
wax models in a large store and fixes on them. On their nippleless
breasts, smooth crutches, round, hard, hemispherical bottoms.
Girls.

The bag on his lap has a tear in it. One of the bottles falls sideways splitting the bag in two. Ritson secures the bottle by its neck, then, putting his thumb over the top of the seal, gently, absent-mindedly, rubs it.

*   *   *

Dissolve through to another thumb rubbing across the top of another bottle, this one open.

It is the Thumb Man. We are in a restaurant. We are awkwardly placed, in that we can only see the Thumb Man from over his left shoulder, and only some of the table. We cannot see the person he is talking to, if indeed he is talking to someone. We hear what he says above subdued restaurant hubbub (it is quite a smart restaurant, unexpectedly smart, for example Rule's in Maiden Lane). The scene takes place in a series of dissolves.

—THE THUMB MAN: I think Russell is on my side. I've squared him. What Payne thinks I don't know. He's very tough. Very ruthless. He's the one to watch. He'll talk the others round if he can. But I'll stand up to him. I can be just as tough—you have to be. I said to him the other day, 'As long as I'm in this position, no-one's muscling in. If I'm sacked, well and good. But until then—no-one's muscling in.' Another one to watch is Jenkins. You have to watch them all, but Jenkins will swing one if he gets a half a chance. I keep my ear to the ground. Play it pretty close to the chest . . .

Dissolve through to the side of the Thumb Man. The bottle is half empty. Throughout the monologue he sips wine.

—THE THUMB MAN: I can take a number 87 to the Tube (that takes five minutes), Tube takes forty minutes with one change, then I have to walk up from the station, that takes ten minutes. Or I can take the BR straight in in thirty-five minutes and walk from there in twenty minutes. I *can* catch a 137 to Oxford Street, which takes thirty minutes, but normally you have to wait eight minutes, and from there a No. 7, or a 15 or a 6 brings you to the door in about seventeen minutes. Or, of course, I can take my car in, though there's the time parking it. In the rush hour I'll be about fifty minutes door to door then five or six minutes parking it. You can see I'm in a bit of a quandary. I can't see any solution . . .

Dissolve through. The bottle is empty. The Thumb man signals a waiter for another one.

—THE THUMB MAN: I don't know, either. It's very difficult to find out who's got the influence, who's in the know. Samuels had a look for a while, he seemed well in. I had a beer with him. Then he got the hoof. That shook me. Last week I thought it was Holmes. This week I'm not sure. It's very hard to find out. It might be Pritchard. I thought I saw him give a sort of nod in the corridor yesterday.

Dissolve through again. The bottle is a third empty.

—THE THUMB MAN: I was mowing the lawn and of course the mower went over my foot. Well, while I was in hospital I thought I might as well have my piles seen to. Then I got an abscess on my tooth—so they did half a dozen fillings at the same time; and while actually *looking* at the piles they found I'd got a small hernia. Managed to nip *that* in the bud, when I fell going to the toilet and cracked my funny bone. All stress diseases, you see.

Dissolve.

—THE THUMB MAN: ... frequently happens now with computers that you get a bill for nine hundred and ninety nine thousand nine hundred and ninety nine pounds. It would be just my luck to get one of those. Of course you don't have to pay, but it would give you quite a turn, the prospect. There was a chap in the papers the other day whose Water Rate was a million pounds. Poor bastard.

Dissolve.

—THE THUMB MAN: ... have you noticed how many men with one arm there are in the streets nowadays?

Dissolve.

—THE THUMB MAN: ... the police ...

Dissolve through again, but this time, although the Thumb Man's lips are moving volubly, we can hear nothing. Just the restaurant hubbub.

*   *   *

Fade and dissolve through to secretaries at lunch. Sparrow chatter, laughter.

—JANICE: He took her to the cinema first and she let him mess about a bit in the back. And afterwards they got into his Ford.

77

Diane said he had this tiny old Ford which was so small she could hardly get her legs in.

—JILL: Most likely an old Anglia. My boy-friend's got one too.

—JANICE: They drove on a bit and then this Indian stopped and they got into the back. Diane said you could hardly get in there either. Well, he messed her about a bit—nothing serious, he never got his dick out. Then he took down her drawers and he licked her raht aht!

—JILL   ⎫
—CHRISTINE ⎬ (surprised, impressed): Raht aht?

—JANICE (with finality): Diane said he licked her raht aht.

Right out. The intonation with which this is said, and the pronunciation, are important. The stress is on 'right'—'raht' or perhaps 'rart'—which should be strong, long-drawn-out and rising. On 'out'—'aht' or 'art'—the note falls and the word is clipped short.

—JILL: You should've seen some of the things that went on in my last office! Honestly, I wasn't sorry to leave. One of the Directors wanted to have me in the lift.

—JANICE: Nothing happens here. It's too big. You never know when someone won't come in. My sister used to work for a publisher. There was this evening when she had to work late and there was no-one else in the office—you wouldn't get that here for a start—and her boy-friend came to see her. He wanted to have her there, at once. She said no, certainly not. You know, it was just cold lino in her office and all full of desks and chairs and typewriters. So he opened the door into the Chairman's office, and said what about here? This has a carpet and lots of room and all. And my sister said she couldn't not in the Chairman's office! In the end they did, had it off right in the middle, and the next morning she went in and there was this stain right on the yellow carpet. She was so embarrassed! She said she thought everyone would notice and guess what it was, so she stood on it to cover it up.

Their voices become like sparrows again. The camera starts to pull back and the sparrow chatter merges through into the twittering of real sparrows. At the same time dissolve through to clouds of birds. After an initial shot of sparrows, pull back to reveal that practically all the birds are pigeons.

*   *   *

The pigeons are whirling, rising, falling, landing, streaming in from all parts of St. James's Park to converge at a single point on the gravel path just off the Mall. In their midst stands Charlie. He is dispensing crumbs from his carrier bag. He throws the crumbs here and there, with forceful, directed movements. The pigeons flutter and beat around him, even, so accustomed are they to this ritual, landing lightly and momentarily on his mackintoshed arms and shoulders.

After a while he walks slowly over to a seat, accompanied St. Francis-like by most of the pigeons of London. He sits down and we can now see his face. His eyes are bright. He looks commanding and amused, dispensing crumbs with judgement—singling out a sparrow, drawing off a large dominant pigeon with a handful so that he can give some to a weaker one. Occasionally he flings crumbs into the air so that the pigeons whirl round his head trying to catch them.

At last the bag is nearly empty. Charlie gets up and sets off towards Admiralty Arch, kicking his way through the thick brown mat of fallen leaves. He looks like a little boy shuffling through the fallen leaves. With his back to the camera, he kicks towards the Arch. Then he puts his right arm into the carrier bag and flings a handful of crumbs out to the flock of pigeons still accompanying him. He moves his arm straight out and up with a jerk like a railway signal. As he repeats the marionette movement again and again, automatically, seeming unaware of it, the camera pulls back and back and back, until Charlie is just a tiny figure in the rain, shuffling through the leaves, jerking his arm up and down, surrounded by pigeons.

*   *   *

A series of quick cuts.

Ellroyd getting into a taxi.

Jessie leaving a Lyons Corner House.

The Thumb Man getting on to a bus.

Lawrence and Chris coming out of a pub.

Anonymous people leaving restaurants, pubs, waving for taxis in the rain, hurrying down pavements, hurrying back into office blocks.

Ellroyd getting out of his taxi and walking into the office.

The same pattern we saw in The Arrival (only not so concerted or definite); the pattern, that is, of a river in reverse: its main stream being continually diminished as dozens of tributaries disappear into doors along the streets.

Finally a long shot of Charlie outside the office, walking slowly up the steps. This, with two exceptions, is the last we shall see of the outside world until The Departure.

THE AFTERNOON

WE are in Miss Hockin's office again. Nothing has altered. Her coat and scarf on the hook, her tea with a saucer on it to keep it warm. The flower she tied up has wilted a bit.

The rain and cloud have made it quite dark. All at once the doors opens, a youth of seventeen strides in, turns on the light and starts to whistle.

He looks round the room, still whistling, then reads a piece of paper in his hand. He looks round the room and walks over to the filing cabinet. He reads the contents list of the top two drawers and then bends to the bottom drawer. He is still looking at his piece of paper.

The camera closes on his hand, poised above the handle. He stops whistling. The hand hangs motionless. Long pause.

The camera pulls back, to show the youth straighten. He resumes whistling. He looks at his paper and walks out to see what is written on the door. It is number 273. He has come to the wrong office. He turns the light off, goes out, shuts the door.

The camera remains for a moment in the empty office, facing the filing cabinet.

*   *   *

Cut to the secretaries dispersing. Sparrow chatter. The notes—high, eager, simultaneous, uncaring—would be exactly the same whether they were talking about the rolls at a Wimpy or the suicide of the assistant accountant.

The camera follows Sue into Bee's office. Bee is standing in front of her mirror, putting the finishing touches to her face. She opens her mouth and examines her teeth.

—BEE (with the air of talking about a catastrophe inevitably on everyone's mind): I'm seeing Bolly at five. We've got to keep them away till then. I don't think they'll try anything. In case he does, I've written this.

She indicates a large sheet of paper which she has folded into a tent so that it stands up on her desk. ON NO ACCOUNT IS THIS DESK TO BE MOVED OR TOUCHED. *Bee Dugdale*.

—BEE: Is it raining?

—SUE: Yes.

Bee takes a flat sausage of plastic out of her large black handbag and slaps it out into a transparent rain hat. She puts it on.

—BEE: You hold the fort while I have a quick lunch. Don't let *anyone* touch the desk. Say you have strict instructions—no, *orders*. It's with a very old gentleman friend as a matter of fact, but I'll be as quick as I can.

She walks out. Though it will be quick, somehow one gathered it will be *intime* too.

*   *   *

The camera follows her as she passes, unseeing, Peter reading a Notice Board. His eyes follow her up the corridor.

He turns and moves slowly in the opposite direction. Beginning-of-the-afternoon restlessness. He opens Bee's door and peers in.

—PETER: Why's Bee so late? Her afternoon lover?

Sue, self-conscious because she knows he knows she 'fancies' him, just smiles and points to Bee's notice.

Peter makes an expression—'oh yes, of course'—shrugs, and goes out, closing the door.

He continues down the corridor in search of entertainment.

He comes to Cyril Wells' and Jessie's office. Jessie is bustling about importantly, even excitedly. Her spectacles swing from their ribbon. Her desk is overflowing with plastic bags.

—PETER (lounging against the door): Going to have a busy afternoon, Jessie?

—JESSIE: Oh yes—quite the busy bee today.

—PETER: What do you need them for?

—JESSIE: Not me. These are for our Cyril.

—PETER: What on earth does he want them all for?

—JESSIE: That he has not vouchsafed.

—PETER: They're getting quite fashionable. I saw Bee Dugdale wearing one in the corridor only a moment ago.

—JESSIE: *À la mode*.

—PETER: Whose idea were they?

—JESSIE: Our Lord and Master—Señor Ellroyd.

—PETER: Really? (Pause.) Tell me—how long's he been here, do you know?

—JESSIE: Since 1956. August 1956. I remember it well. That was the month that Invoice Servicing first came into my life. We used to be in Accounts, you know.

—PETER: Did you really? How fascinating.

He watches her put a gleaming heap of plastic bags on to her desk. They slither to the floor.

—PETER: What on earth can Cyril want with all those bags?

—JESSIE (coming from her cupboard with another armful): Ours not to reason why . . .

—PETER: Perhaps he's going to give an absolutely *enormous* picnic . . .

Dissolve through to Peter wandering down the corridor.

He looks into several offices. Lawrence is sitting alone in his, at his desk. The desk has been swept bare, everything put into drawers.

—LAWRENCE (exaggerated warmth): Come and sit down, Peter. Here, let me get you a chair.

—PETER: Thank you, dear. I can't find anyone in to talk to.

—LAWRENCE: Restless?

—PETER: It's such awful weather. I had lunch in my office for the first time in my life. Have you ever done it? It's just like the war. Pilchards' heads.

—LAWRENCE: I meant these office afternoons. The central heating. They get one down. I don't know . . .

—PETER: Don't they drag *on*. I could scream.

—LAWRENCE (unable to contain himself): I've decided to leave. I'm resigning this afternoon or tomorrow.

—PETER: You're not! Goodness! Why? More money I suppose. Have you got another job?

—LAWRENCE: I have. Yes. But . . .

He stands up while talking so that he can look into the In Tray by the door.

—LAWRENCE: I'm not sure that I'll take it now. I think I ought to cut loose for a while. Experiment with something new.

—PETER: How bold. What sort of thing?

—LAWRENCE (leaning forward): I thought a few of us might try it together. For instance—what about an Ideas Group?

—PETER: Have you any ideas, dear? I . . .

—LAWRENCE (sweeping on): I was thinking on the lines of a

83

Ministry of all the Talents. I was wondering if you'd like to join? Bainbridge is very bright. Me. There's a friend I had at Reading—Jonty . . .

—PETER (hastily): I'd be no good at all, dear. I never have ideas.

—LAWRENCE (leaning back): But seriously, Peter—you don't mind me asking you this do you?—haven't you ever thought of leaving? Doesn't it ever cross your mind.

—PETER: Sometimes. At 3.30 in the morning. I'm simply terrified.

—LAWRENCE: Don't be. Honestly. You should take the plunge. It's . . . (Pause.) These last few weeks have been a revelation to me.

—PETER: I'm sometimes terrified that for no reason at all—you know, to visit Corfu or something—I shall suddenly find I've given it up. A fit of madness. And there it'd be—*gone*!

—LAWRENCE: But you can't *like* it? You know, I've come to realise . . . (Pause.) It's not until you give it up that you realise how much you've hated it, how much you've repressed. (Pause, matter-of-fact.) I've found I've hated it for years.

—PETER: In that case, dear, you're very wise to go.

—LAWRENCE (musing): The triviality. (Pause.) Trapped for one's whole life—office talk, office tea, office smell. (Bursting out.) You can't *possibly* like it, Peter? You don't *enjoy* it, look *forward* to it, I mean . . .? (He spreads his hands.)

—PETER: Most certainly I do. I love nearly every minute.

—LAWRENCE: Why?

—PETER: I like the cosiness for one thing.

—LAWRENCE: You mean safe? Secure? You can't *just* want to be safe, for Christ's sake. Have you no other reasons?

—PETER: I certainly do want to be safe. I don't want to live a life of danger. I'm not the type, dear. Besides—I like it.

—LAWRENCE: Why?

—PETER: Oh, what a bore. Do you really want me to tell you?

—LAWRENCE: Yes.

Initially impatient, Peter quite quickly gets interested in what he is saying; at the end almost carried away.

—PETER: Well, frankly I think it's rather a silly question. I would have thought it was obvious. For one thing, there's all the gossip. You've heard about the fuss Bee's making over her desk, I

84

daresay. Apparently Betty Piggott has been having an affair with Leslie Elliott for *five years*. I suppose you'd call that trivial. But triviality depends on your point of view. I find it quite absorbing.

And then it's so dramatic. Do you remember when that little man with a beard scrambled on to a water tank or cupboard or wherever it was in the Ladies loo on the fifth floor? I thought I'd die of excitement. I will tell you one thing. I don't really *like* too much real life any more. I'm quite ready to admit it. In the office you get little dramas, little friendships, little loves and hates. With one or two additions which we won't go into, my entire emotional life is satisfied here.

—LAWRENCE: Yes, but this is a very small part of office life, isn't it?

—PETER: What do you mean small? It *is* office life. In fact for a great many people it is *life*. What seems to you small may be satisfying really deep needs.

For instance I am very easily bored. Bat squeaks of boredom go through me the whole time. In an office I can always leave, move on to some other subject, get away.

Another thing, I have to have an almost continuous flow of conversation. It doesn't really matter how superficial. Here everyone has the same terms of reference. That's extremely important. I can go into any office on four floors and they'll be electrified that you're leaving. The office is the only place where I feel liberated. It's the only place, for example—the only time in my life—where I can effortlessly transcend class barriers.

—LAWRENCE (barely suppressing impatience): But, Peter—the *work*. I enjoy a bit of gossip as much as the next man. But the appalling triviality of the work; the monotony of it, the undemandingness of it. You might as well spend the rest of your life . . . I don't know . . . piling up pins or something. Balancing tiddlywinks in heaps.

—PETER: Well, let's be practical, dear. If we didn't work in an office, what would we do? Oddly enough, I have rather a lot of energy, inherited from my mother. I'm not creative. I can't write. I certainly couldn't be a labourer. Doctor? Barrister? Politician? I can't see myself being any of those. Willy-nilly, it's an office for me I fear.

You say it's undemanding—but that's the whole point. It's the defects of British business that makes it such a delightful life. I can't *understand* those cries for efficiency and so on. They appal me. We're still in the Pastoral Age of business, a business Arcadia, which these people are trying to destroy. I hope they fail. Every day I do my best to ensure that they will. If I had my way the emphasis would be quite the other way round: Business *In*efficiency Exhibitions, Cost *In*effectiveness courses ...

—LAWRENCE: But the endless competition, the struggling to get approval, the degrading sucking up. The stupid battles to get one's way. The ruthlessness.

PETER: Not in Specifications ducky. And who's ruthless in Packaging and Design? No-one's been sacked for fifteen years. In America perhaps. Not here. It was even better before the war I don't doubt, but it's still Arcadia. In any case, even in America, competitiveness is human nature. You can't blame offices. No—I thought it was triviality you were complaining about.

—LAWRENCE: Well, it is. I meant it. I know it's a relief that people don't push us too hard, perhaps it's not so ruthless. But honestly, Peter, you can't deny it's trivial, footling, year after year the same footling, bloody boring, pointless little things. You're not being serious?

—PETER: I'm perfectly serious, dear. The trouble with you is you can't see things in human terms. You see things in the abstract. It's rather chilling.

Look, take me. I suffer from mild morning depression, you know. How would I get out of it without the office?

I want you to try and imagine it from my point of view. Imagine what I'm like. I get fearfully worried if my mother moves my toothbrush. I always come to work by the same route—well, occasionally a change, accompanied by instant anxiety.

So what happens? I arrive and find a little pile of familiar, easy, what you'd call trivial work. The pleasure of settling down to it! I begin to feel calm. I forget myself. It's like tapestry; time passes, the mind is active or drifts, distant sounds of—you know—the tinkle of the tea trolley, the ping of a typewriter bell.

It's like Vivaldi. It's an initial subjective reaction. If you like it, every variation is fascinating, however small. You know what I mean—there are tiny nuances within the repetition. Take leaden afternoons like this, when the rain is falling on bored buildings, so many bored buildings. Today there's a feeling of *universal* boredom, a great *brotherhood* of boredom. I find it very warming.

And don't you love autumn? I come by exactly the same route of course, but London seems to me to have changed. It feels like a huge public school or university. There's a smell of ink in the air.

It's a love of small things. I can remember my tables at my prep school when I got into the Senior Common Room. Did you have the same? One was allowed to make a little niche for oneself—two or three tables and some wall, with oneself in the middle. All one's possessions spread about. I can remember the layout of it all now.

And it's the same with work, a letter comes. I answer it. He raises a query. I answer it and raise one myself. Finally, all is settled and we thank each other. Or there are some details about screws; a question of patent infringement. I have to re-read the laws on patents and copyright, redefine it to myself for the five hundredth time, look up what Tankard and Baggott have to say. I *never* tire of Tankard and Baggott. There's always some subtlety one's missed or forgotten. I keep their book on my desk. You may have noticed it on the left next to the paper clip tin. I read it. Outside it's raining. In a minute I shall go and find out exactly *what* Cyril can have needed all those bags for. Do you see what I mean?

It's really a question of the small canvas. People who do *petit-point* and who get absorbed in thousands of small stitches. Or *trompe d'œil*. I think in a way it may be for people who want to stay in the nursery. Certainly I've found myself thinking of the office as I ride towards it as a large squat nanny, waiting comfortably there to gently fuss me with all the details of her tiny, cosy world.

In essence it's a question of temperament, don't you agree? A question of artistic temperament. You—of *course*, I'd never realised before—there's something swashbuckling about you, Van Gogh. You've never been tamed. Whereas me—I'm a miniaturist, a Tailor of Gloucester.

Long pause. Peter apparently unconcerned, but watching Lawrence. Lawrence staring grimly, conscientiously, at his hands.

—LAWRENCE (frank, honest smile, admitting his weakness—or strength): No. Sorry, Peter. It's no good. I can't take it.

A flicker of irritation (or disappointment) crosses Peter's face. Pause. Lawrence leans forward very earnestly.

—LAWRENCE: The thing is, I've never been *used*. I feel I've never been fully *stretched*.

—PETER: Haven't you, dear?

87

The door opens and a boy comes in.

—BOY: Mr. Gurney?

—LAWRENCE: Yes?

—BOY: Mr. Ellroyd wants to see you right away.

—LAWRENCE (rising slowly, controlled nerves): The Vice Chairman? Does he? I'll be up right away.

—PETER: Good luck. Will you resign?

—LAWRENCE (pausing by the door to glance into the still empty In Tray): I don't know. I'll probably leave it till tomorrow. Don't tell anyone till I tell you, will you?

—PETER: No.

Lawrence strides out. Peter stands up and strolls over to Lawrence's desk. He has one hand in his pocket. He goes round behind the desk and leaning forward opens the drawers one after another, shutting one before opening the next. It is now we learn that Lawrence's desk, apparently so neat and clean, is in a state of complete internal chaos. Papers, files, bits of plastic, half sheets, torn, of Letraset, biros, bills, a notebook, are crammed into the drawers. The contents almost burst out. Tucked down in one drawer is an old piece of sandwich. In another, cigarette ash.

Although Peter is presumably just looking briefly through these drawers out of superficial curiosity, we get the feeling that they are in fact being presented to us. A drawer is opened, the camera holds on it, the drawer is shut. The same with the next drawer. And the next. In some odd way Peter has become the *deux en machina*; for an instant not himself but a chorus, a silent narrator, the spirit of The Office. It gives us a cold, strange feeling, not pleasant; the sort of feeling Cocteau was so good at arousing in his films.

Peter walks slowly up Lawrence's office, both hands in his pockets. He goes out of the door, a step or so along the corridor and we follow him into Bob Glenny's studio.

*　　*　　*

Bob, Ray and Geoffrey are standing round the Display Piece looking at it hard and in silence. Peter walks towards them.

—BOB: I've a notion we may need a bit of a border here. Nothing too fancy. Something firm.

—RAY: To pull it together?

—BOB: Yes. Round here. A bit of come-hither.

—PETER (diffidently): A decorative border, you mean?

—BOB: Oh, hello there, Peter. Yes. You can see we have a bit of a problem here. (Slowly, professionally.) It's a bit all-over-the-place at the moment. No come-hither. My notion is a border, or a border motif, might pull it together.

—PETER: Well, I don't want to interfere and I'm sure he'll tell you himself but actually Lawrence was thinking along the same lines.

—BOB: Lawrence was?

—PETER: Yes. I was just having a chat with him and he happened to mention he'd had an idea for a Display. I must say I thought it very fetching, but I'm sure he'll tell you himself.

—BOB: I'd be interested to know now if I could. I want to get this out of the way and we could be getting on with it.

Peter leans forward and points with one long finger.

—PETER: Well, what he thought—and I did think it was striking—was a frieze of bottoms.

—BOB (Pause): What?

—PETER: A frieze, or fringe, if you like, of naked bottoms—quite a new departure Lawrence felt.

—BOB: Arses?

—PETER: Yes. Of course you could vary them; some big, some pinched and tiny, hair or not, old, or young, *jeune bottoms en fleur*. Or just have a straight repetition of the same bottom. In a way perhaps that would be best. Very simple. Very strong. It would give you bags of come-hither.

Bob has turned very red. He opens his mouth. For a moment we think he may be going to laugh.

—BOB (bursting out): I shan't do it! I've never heard anything like it! I've been in this business twenty-nine years. I have professional pride. I shall refuse to do it. It's the most ridiculous thing I've ever heard in my life.

—PETER: Oh, I don't know.

—BOB: I know this is a so-called permissive age, but there are limits. You've got to take a stand. This will shock people. Think of the associations for one thing. They'll rub off on our product. I shall take this straight to the Sales Director. Right away. I've no choice.

—PETER: Really, Bob, it's only a joke.

—BOB (voice rising): A joke?

—PETER: I was joking. Naturally Lawrence would never

dream of such a thing. As a matter of fact he never mentioned the Display at all.

—BOB (recategorising): A joke. I see. A joke.

—PETER: I didn't mean to upset you. Good heavens, look at the time! I must fly.

He hurries out. We just hear Bob begin, 'All the same, the very idea . . .' and then we are in the corridor.

*   *   *

The afternoon is thoroughly under way. People are bustling to and fro. It can now be assumed that the viewer is familiar with the various elements that have been introduced—Charlie in the lift, the office décor, etc.—and there is no need for the camera to emphasise them any more. Only new elements, or new additions to old elements (as, for instance, with the Thumb Man), receive this attention.

Cyril is reading some notices on the Notice Board, rising rapidly up and down on his toes. Three men in dirty white boiler suits are pushing a large new desk against the wall outside Bee's door. (It is just about identical to the one she has already.)

The camera follows Peter. We see Lawrence coming towards us. They stop.

—PETER: What happened?

—LAWRENCE: Nothing. He didn't have time to see me, after all. His meeting ran on and then he had to go to a Board meeting. I've got to go and see him at four o'clock.

*   *   *

Cut to Bolton coming out of his office. He has on a clean shirt and a different suit. An inch-long strip of Elastoplast on his forehead is the only sign of his morning's ordeal. He is rather drunk; face red and congested, head lowered. A dangerous mood.

The camera follows him down the corridor. At the end is a mahogany door with the words Board Room embossed on it in gold. Bolton opens the door and walks in.

Four Directors are standing about talking; Ellroyd and three others whose faces we will have seen earlier, among the arriving crowds or in the corridors, but whose names we don't know or need to know. The Board Room is large and airy, long polished table with pads and pencils, modern abstracts on the walls, an expensive clock, etc.

Bolton stands near the group of Directors, glowering and humming. One of them turns politely to him.

—DIRECTOR 1: Hello, Woodrow.

—BOLTON: What? (Hums.)

—DIRECTOR 1: Appalling weather. It's really getting quite cold out.

—BOLTON (truculently): I feel like going out and killing a baby.

He stares straight up at the Director, humming. The Director gives an uneasy laugh.

—DIRECTOR 1: I know what you mean. Ha ha ha ha ha ha. Oh dear . . .

Bolton turns away, still humming. He goes up to Ellroyd.

—BOLTON: What are we waiting for? I've got a lot to do this afternoon.

—ELLROYD: Cameron. I can't understand it. He asked for the meeting to be brought forward.

—BOLTON: Cameron chose this ungodly hour, did he?

—ELLROYD (to Director 2): Donald—give Cameron a ring, will you? See what's up.

—BOLTON (humming loudly): Hmmmmmm Hmmmmmm Pom Pom Pom Hmmmm zip-a-de-do-da-pom.

The door opens and Cameron, Company Secretary, glides in. He is tall and distinguished, with thick greying hair, a prominent Nasser nose, close-set eyes, tufty eyebrows and those Master-of-Foxhounds tuffets on each cheek bone.

—CAMERON (having to speak above Bolton's humming and pom-pomming, which increases): I'm so sorry, gentlemen. I was delayed. If you'd like to begin, Mr. Bolton . . .?

—BOLTON: Why are we meeting at this appalling hour?

—CAMERON: It was the only time we could get Vavaslar Vivenchki. I think I mentioned . . .

—BOLTON: What on earth do we need an expert for? The thing's as plain as the nose on your face.

—CAMERON: I hope you're right, sir. Providence, I learnt at two forty-five has delayed Comrade Vivenchki in Prague. We shall have to do without him.

—BOLTON: This is a ridiculous time to hold a Board meeting. I don't suppose anyone's sober. I'm certainly not sober. ⟨

91

The Directors have been sitting down during this conversation, which Bolton has held fairly loudly but ostensibly with Cameron, striding up and down, Cameron soothing and discreet beside him. Bolton sits at the head of the table and looks round.

—BOLTON: Where's everyone else? We can't begin yet. There's no-one here.

—CAMERON: We have a quorum, sir.

—BOLTON: Quorum—Bore-um. No wonder they're called Bored meetings—they're so boring. Ha ha ha ha ha. Nothing of any importance was ever decided by a Bore-um.

All right, let's begin. The Accountant's report first, middle-Europe last. Who wants to sound off.

The Directors are used to Bolton, but they can still be embarrassed by him and frightened of him.

The camera closes on his face—dissolves into it so that we see the next few sequences through his eyes. Not just from his position, but actually through his eyes. That is, a fuzzed ridge must be lowered and raised across the screen as he half closes and opens his eyes; faces blur; once he squints sideways and looks at his nose, very large, close and indistinct; three or four times he nearly falls asleep and a vast lid sinks down producing, not darkness, but that reddened opaque screen of lightly shut eyes. Similarly we hear it through his ears: a continuous, almost meaningless drone most of the time, the sound of his breathing, the traffic. Occasionally, quietly, he hums. From time to time words, sentences penetrate this Bolton wild track and twice he jerks awake and speaks.

—DIRECTOR 3: ... backed by the name of this firm with all that that implies.

—BOLTON (starting up): *What* does it imply?

—DIRECTOR 3: Why—good-quality workmanship. Prompt delivery. Guaranteed satisfaction. The best. In a word—everything we stand for. Wouldn't you agree?

—BOLTON: No, I would not. Rubbish. You talk like that man from our Agency—what's his name. The 'best' indeed. We're not Rolls-Royce. We're not even a household name. The most we can hope is that a few people associate us with *some* of our products.

—DIRECTOR 3 (stung): Frankly, Mr. Bolton——

He has lost Bolton's attention. The lid descends. Bolton's stomach rumbles. Traffic. A few sentences emerge, though we see little or nothing.

—ELLROYD: What's this term Double Accounting, Donald? Does it mean we have two bites at the cherry.

—DIRECTOR 2: That's more or less the story.

—ELLROYD: If you mean two bites at the cherry I wish you'd say two bites at the cherry. It's so much simpler.

—DIRECTOR 2: Actually it's more like *three* bites at the cherry. The computer twice, then a third time—humanly.

—ELLROYD (his voice already fading, becoming a dream): I suppose the ideal would be a thousand bites at the cherry . . .

Mumble mumble. Traffic. Drone. Then abruptly the lid shoots up, the screen clears, the camera pulls back, an observer again.

—BOLTON: Eastern Europe? I thought you were going to get in an expert, Cameron?

—CAMERON: I'm sorry, sir. I tried to explain. Mr. Vivenchki is delayed at Prague.

—BOLTON (forceful, if slurred and rambling with only apparent non sequiturs): We need an expert. This isn't the sort of decision that should be taken after a heavy lunch. I had prepared a statement but I've forgotten it. But I'll let Jack here take over. He knows my view. (Pause.) Besides, it's a foreign question. I think I should tell you I may have second thoughts. *Second thoughts.* I *may* decide to remain on in charge of Internal and Domestic policy. Jack here would take over the Foreign and Export side. A joint Chairmanship. Could work very well, very well. I'm finding a lot of things here that no-one else seems able to manage. None of you have my nose for significant detail. (Pause.) Have any of you read Crack and Wilson on the Double Helix?

Pause. They look at him blankly. At length

—DIRECTOR 2: Isn't it *Crick* and Wilson, Woodrow?

—BOLTON: Crack, Crick, Crock—what does it matter? The point was they had these Ribosomes of something—RBA. One day Crack noticed something odd about them, can't remember what. Say he noticed the Ribosomes smelt of onions. Something apparently quite insignificant, but he followed it up, followed it up, worried it out and in the end—bang! The Double Helix! Or it might *not* have been the Double Helix. The point was he *found out.*

That reminds me. The expense of Eastern Europe would be trifling. A man in Rumania or somewhere, going around to Trade Fairs and making contacts. Probably for five years without any result. But the markets could be vast. They prefer to deal with

93

individual capitalist sods like ourselves than with Governments. If they don't turn West and Russia can hold them—we lose nothing. If they do—we may gain a hell of a lot. All we need is Cameron's expert to tell us how to set about it, start us on the right lines, get us some contacts. Pay him a retainer.

Pause. He stands up.

—BOLTON: Will you still have a Bore-um if I go, Cameron?

—CAMERON: Yes, Mr. Bolton, if you'll——

—BOLTON (testily): Yes, yes, I know. Jack, take the Chair will you. I've got some work to do.

He walks out. The Directors rise and half rise. The camera follows Bolton out of the door.

*　　　*　　　*

Cut to Cyril Wells. He is reading a notice on the board outside the Thumb Man's office. He rises slowly up and down on his toes.

He reads (and the camera closes on the notice):

'It is with deep regret that I have to announce the death in the Thurston Road Hospital, Wimbledon, of Derek Reeves. Derek served the Company loyally and well for over twenty-four years. He joined as a messenger in 1938 and after the war rose swiftly to become a valuable and trusted member of No. 6 Processing Group. He was promoted Under Manager in 1956 and served in that position for twelve years until his tragically early death this week.

He leaves a widow and one child. The funeral will be on Wednesday at 3 p.m. at St. Mary's Church, Church Road, Wimbledon. Gwen Reeves would like all flowers sent to the church. The Board, with what I know are the heartfelt condolences of the whole firm, has sent a wreath in the name of us all.'

Cyril walks away and the camera, as it were shifted by this, moves to rest on the door of the Thumb Man's office.

*　　　*　　　*

Dissolve through. We are behind the Thumb Man (the impression must be that we are spying on him). The camera rests on him. Pause. The Thumb Man reaches down to the bottom right-hand drawer (without looking), pulls it open and takes out a bottle of whisky. He half fills a plastic cup, also in the drawer, drinks, then replaces cup and bottle and shuts the drawer. Before these movements are quite complete we cut to . . .

*   *   *

. . . Ritson's office. It is beginning to grow dark, gloomy. When they notice they'll turn on the light. Martin is alone, desultorily working. After a pause, Ritson comes slowly in and takes off his soaking mackintosh, gives it a half-hearted shake and lays it across the filing cabinet. He sits down and rubs his face in his hands. Then he sits staring at his desk, hands cupped round his face. Long pause.

—MARTIN (dryly): *Post coitum omnium tristes est.*

—RITSON: Not usually. (Pause.) I don't know, I think I'll have to pack it up.

—MARTIN: Up?

—RITSON: In. Out. Whatever the word is. Stop it all.

—MARTIN: Could you?

—RITSON: God knows. Now I think so. I suppose in an hour or so . . . But it's getting me down.

—MARTIN: It certainly gets *me* down. I feel such a failure when you come back from . . . well, when you come back like this in the middle of the afternoon. It makes me feel quite impotent. I suppose I *am* a failure really. (Pause.) You usually say at least it keeps you young.

—RITSON (wearily): I know you think I just show off to you. A middle-aged show-off. I promise you it's not that. (Pause.) Keeps me young. That's the trouble. Imagine still having the preoccupations of an adolescent when you're forty-five. It's revolting.

—MARTIN: I don't know about revolting exactly . . .

—RITSON (roughly, lighting his cigarette, a bit drunk): Oh, for Christ's sake—imagine it. You know when you were sixteen and you suddenly got an erection in Geography class and had to put up your hand and go to the bog to toss off? Or didn't dare stand up in the bus because of the bulge in your trousers? Remember? Feeling randy just about the whole time. I'm like that now—still. It's a bloody treadmill. Endlessly the same obsession, on and on.

95

I'm the failure. I'm an experiment in over-developing one instinct, one appetite—and it's failed, it doesn't work.

—MARTIN: It's not exactly the first time the experiment's been made. Some people like it. At least you have an aim.

—RITSON: Aim! For Christ's sake, what an aim! It's not an aim—it's a disease. A fever. And it gets worse. I used to want something like one out of every ten women. Now it's more like one in five. Sometimes it's every woman under fifty. And quite a lot over fifty.

—MARTIN: Even the ugly ones?

—RITSON: *Especially* the ugly ones often. Liking sex is nothing to do with looks. I remember I once had (pause) . . . doesn't matter. No—I think of those sexy ugly ones all frustrated, boiling over, wanting to touch themselves up. A really ugly woman—Christ. Some days *anything* excites me. (Pause.) There I go again. Stirring it up. (Sighs.) No, it's not that. Honestly, Martin—think of it. It's not an aim. I don't suppose I've read twenty books in the last five years. I can't remember when I last went to a concert. I don't even know these girls. The whole thing's so superficial. I hardly know Pam, for instance, though I've had her dozens of times. She's waiting there now. I don't really know any of them—it's just breasts, and cunts and bottoms and mouths, endlessly. Tits, cunts, bottoms, mouths. No friends. No peace. I never think. I don't read, listen to music.

—MARTIN: You make it sound rather heroic.

—RITSON (laughs): I got carried away. But honestly—I do sometimes think what a bloody waste it is. At my age, just to be thinking of the next girl and the next and the next *ad infinitum*.

—MARTIN: Most people think about them but can't get them. But (slowly) yes—number does seem to play a part. I wonder . . .

—RITSON: What?

—MARTIN: I mean the conventional interpretation would be not so much it was an instinct, I mean too much instinct, which is rather flattering really, but that you were just trying to prove something, that you weren't queer or weren't impotent or as good as your father or something. It's an explanation I'd prefer.

—RITSON: You may be right. I don't know. I only know I find myself revolting sometimes. Often.

—MARTIN: Don't tell me you can still feel guilty?

—RITSON: For Christ's sake—of course I feel guilty. I told you this morning. You're always asking if I feel guilty. It's not too bad talking to you now, tight. But this evening ... (Pause.) You haven't been a Catholic. Do you know we had to confess every single time we masturbated? I never stopped. Five or six times a night. I was going to write a book, *My Mistress was a Mattress* by Miles the Marvellous Masturbator. No truly—don't raise your eyebrows. I'm not trying to boast. I was made to feel guilty every time. 'Bless me Father for I have sinned.' I'm not sure it didn't create a pattern. There's another explanation for you—the need for guilt. All I know is I *do* feel guilty. I feel a real shit when I slink back to Angela, or stagger back drunk and stinking. And the children. I never see enough of them. That makes me guilty. Poor girl, stuck down there with five children. I try and make it up—and then of course it just happens again. I don't know why she still loves me.

—MARTIN (lightly): Women love us for our weaknesses.

—RITSON: It depends on the weakness. They often love us despite our weaknesses.

—MARTIN: Perhaps Anne loves me because my weakness is being too weak to give way to the weakness I'd like to give way to.

Ritson gets up slowly and turns on the single overhead light and the electric fire. He pulls files towards him.

—RITSON: Come on—we're not getting anywhere like this. If I'm to see Ellroyd this afternoon we must get this sorted out. I'll probably need another drink to get through that.

*   *   *

Cut to a lavatory on the sixth floor. Six stand-up urinals (of the basin variety), five cubicles, four with doors open, one door shut, a mirror along one wall. In front of this is an Executive, thirty-four, combing his hair. His thick florid face, his body, give the impression of containing too much blood. He blows out his lips, combs his thick, short hair; pug eyes, regard pug face with unconscious approval, almost love.

—EXECUTIVE (rather loudly, deliberately): *I—made—a—bloody—fuss.* You could tell it was rabbit. I know rabbit from chicken. The bloody waiter said the bones were chicken bones. So they were. But as I pointed out, nothing's easier than to stick a few chicken bones in among the rabbit, is there? I can tell you, I made a bloody fuss.

He finishes combing and looks at his profile.

—EXECUTIVE: Robin? (Pause.) Robin? (Pause.) Are you going to stay there all afternoon?

Pause. He walks over to the cubicle with the shut door, looks at it, then pushes it. The door swings open. The cubicle is empty.

—EXECUTIVE: Slunk off!

Four young men come in laughing and talking. The Executive's face registers their arrival. After an instant's hesitation he continues into the cubicle as though that had been his purpose. The camera is beside him, at seat height; because of the confined space, of necessity in close-up. He turns round, takes down his trousers and sits on the lavatory. His trousers and pants are round his ankles. After a while he begins to whistle.

                           *   *   *

Cut to a long shot of Bee's corridor. This cut, in common with the last three, employs none of the usual link-ups. Nor, on the whole, will subsequent cuts. Familiarity may now be beginning to lull the viewer into forgetting, or at least not noticing, the essential nature of The Office. It is arbitrary, unrelated, indifferent and impersonal. It appears to be an organism, to have a 'spirit'; but in fact it is just a theatre of events, without a heart or a mind. The unrelated nature of the cuts, the lack of those linking associations which, in a film, give an impression of a whole, will henceforward serve to emphasise the disintegrated aspect of offices, one of the most important and unpleasant things about them.

Cut to a long shot of Bee's corridor. Bee appears at her door and looks left and right. Suddenly she bends and tries with all her force to push the desk outside her door down the corridor. She strains for several moments. The desk does not move. At last she straightens, face red, hair a little dishevelled, and disappears into her office again.

Cyril Wells is coming down the corridor, board and bull-dog clip in hand. Peter, now in view to the left of the screen, watches him approach. The camera closes.

—PETER: Busy afternoon, Cyril?

—CYRIL (starting): Oh, not too bad. Quite a lot to do. A lot on.

—PETER: Did you have a nice picnic?

—CYRIL: What?

—PETER: You and all your friends. It must have been quite a sight—the field of the plastic bag.

—CYRIL (nervously uncomprehending): Oh, some picnic, ha ha ha. Ha ha ha—it's no picnic. (He puts on, unexpectedly, a stage Indian voice.) Oh, my goodness, no. Oh, my goodness, no. Ha ha ha ha. (Resumes his own voice again.) Actually, seriously, Peter—it *is* no picnic. I—well it's now becoming fairly urgent I imagine. The Vice Chairman gave me an instruction this morning, a personal directive. You don't happen to know a Mr. Ritson, do you? The (he leafs through his board) the Sales Manager for B Division. I can't locate him.

—PETER: Never heard of him, ducky. Ask Reception.

—CYRIL: Ah! Ho! Good idea. Excellent. Thank goodness. Ah.

*   *   *

Cut to the attic area under the roof. It is pitch-dark. The same noises of water cisterns, lift shafts, etc., with, now, the sound of the rain.

In the distance we see a pencil beam of light. The camera closes.

Mr. Bolton is studying a plan of the roof area. Numerous other plans are rolled up under his arm. After a moment he sets off into the roof, the pencil beam picking out an inadequate path. He blunders into and over debris, old chairs, a roll of flex etc. He mutters and swears.

He reaches a trap door. Grunting with pleasure, breathing heavily, he pulls it open and climbs down the steps it reveals.

He is arriving on a short landing at the top of a staircase. A distinguished-looking grey-haired man stands watching him descend. Bolton stops at the bottom of the steps, hardly glancing at the man, and unfurls another plan. He studies it.

—MAN: Do you mind telling me what you are doing in our roof?

—BOLTON (continuing to study the plan): What?

—MAN: I said will you please tell me what you've been doing in our roof.

Running down the wall beside the stairs, coming through the ceiling from the roof area, is the extractor shaft. But instead of the battered, leaking, cob-webbed thing it is above, now it is encased

99

respectably in wood and painted to match the wall. Bolton looks up from his plan and sees it. His eyes gleam. He rolls up the plan, tucks it into the others under his arm and advances to the stairs.

—BOLTON (thrusting past the man): Get out of my way.

He sets off down the stairs.

—MAN (loudly): I'm afraid I can't let you go like that you know. I insist on an explanation. Stop. Come here . . .

He sets off down the stairs after Mr. Bolton. The camera accompanies him. After two flights the staircase is barred by a door through which Mr. Bolton has evidently just passed. Above it is written: *Manganese Oxygen Holdings Ltd*. The man stops in front of this, perplexed, a stickleback at the boundary of another stickleback's territory. He makes one or two vague gestures of entering. Eventually he turns round and goes up the stairs again.

Cut to Mr. Bolton. He is at a point in the offices of Manganese Oxygen Holdings Ltd., where the extractor shaft disappears into the floor. He is kneeling beside it, a plan spread out in front of him.

—BOLTON: Now. Let me see.

A tall, attractive secretary appears behind him.

—SECRETARY: Can I help?

—BOLTON (looking up): Yes. Look, if Braine's damned plans are accurate I think we must be here.

*　　*　　*

Cut to a head in profile, a black silhouette filling half the screen. Beyond this black, sharp profile (and below it. The owner must be standing at the top of some steps) we see the Post and Dispatch section. This is a large basement hall, brightly lit by neon. It is a miniature post office sorting room. Franking machines, racks for letters, down the middle men packing, sorting, stamping. There is endless bustle.

But we see this in long shot. It's only half in focus, the impression is of bright light with indistinct movements going on.

The camera is to one side of the head that dominates the screen. This head, in deep shadow, might be that of some Aztec warrior. It is motionless. It could be an ancient Mexican statue, a single famous frame preserved from Eisenstein's *Quo Vadis*. We

100

are looking down, past the silhouetted statue of Tococec, into the hot flaring desert of central Andelrapanos; black shadowed god, white sand and heat.

The statue moves slightly so that, more full face, it comes into the light. It raises and drinks from a mug of tea. It is Charlie. He lowers his mug and continues staring down into Dispatch. The camera closes still more. We are near his eye. We notice, in the light from Dispatch (which is now even more fuzzed and out of focus) the embryonic qualities of Charlie's head and face. It does, indeed, floating above the vague shapes and shadows of Despatch, for a moment resemble the embryo at the end of Stanley Kubrick's *Space Odyssey*.

* * *

Cut to a quick shot, in close-up, of the Thumb Man filling his glass with whisky, drinking it, replacing glass, shutting the drawer.

* * *

Cut to Bee's office. The little lamp on her desk, with its gay shade, is on. So is a tall standard lamp, an aluminium pole, beside the armchair. The lights have come on all over the building and we have reached that point when it is not only impossible to get out of the office but even impossible to see out. When we look out we only see ourselves looking in. The cameras can therefore now face the rain-streaked windows directly.

Bee is sitting at her desk, taking off her make-up with sweeps of cold-cream-covered balls of cotton wool. Peter is in the armchair, swinging his leg.

—BEE: God knows what he's been up to all day. He's obviously had one of his hunches. The only time I can see him is at five fifteen. Still—we'll soon sort it out. (Pause.) You think I'm making too much fuss, don't you *Pierre*?

—PETER: I know it must be maddening. I don't even like it when they move my stapling machine dusting. But it is only a *desk*, dear, it's not as though . . .

—BEE: You don't know this place like I do. Were you here with Charles Robinson? A smasher. But lazy. Very vague. First they took his name off the telephone list. Then they removed his

101

typewriter. Finally he had no desk and no name on his door. Just a chair. He hadn't the faintest idea who he was or anything, or what to do. He wandered about. I believe he didn't even have a telephone. In the end they took away the chair and he had a complete nervous breakdown.

—PETER: But, Bee darling, they're trying to *give* you a desk.

—BEE (throwing handfulls of used cotton wool balls into her waste-paper basket): It's how these things begin. I told you I had a little brush with Jack Ellroyd this morning? (Peter nods.) He's never liked me. He'd like to get rid of me. I'm the last of the Old Guard. It's part of a pattern.

She starts to make up her face. Pause.

—BEE: Anyway—it's a question of principle. There was no consultation. They just rode roughshod over me. It's taken me years to get this office up to this pitch. Those reproductions. My armchair. Two waste-paper baskets. This desk was getting quite a patina. (She strokes the desk with her fingers. Her voice rises.) And then they thrust themselves in. Typically masculine—no sensitivity or any idea how a woman feels.

—PETER (rising): Bee dear, don't worry. It will be perfectly all right. I'm sure they'll take it away.

—BEE (rising, laughing, a note of hysteria): Could we move it together? The horrible great thing. It weighs a ton. Perhaps we could push it out of a window. That would be wonderful. That's why something had to be done about Charles Robinson. He threw a typewriter out of the window. Anyway—it would do terrible damage. It would smash a bus to smithereens. The horrid thing.

—PETER: I must go, dear. Give me a ring if you need me.

—BEE: You're so sweet to listen and help. I will. If those great men come again I'll ring you at once. I think I'll try and get them to shift it again. Mr. Braine won't speak to me now. I gave him a piece of my mind.

Pause. Peter waves from the door and goes out. Bee stands thinking. Then, still trembling a little, she lifts the internal telephone. Dials.

—BEE: Is he there? (Pause.) Bee Dugdale. (Pause.) No, I thought not. Well, please give him this message. I want his horrid desk removed from outside my office at once. It's completely blocking the passage. No-one can get in or out. They have to clamber over it.

* * *

102

Cut to Lawrence's office. Chris is working. Janice is typing. Lawrence is sitting impassively, arms straight out, both palms flat on his bare desk. He is looking at the In Tray.

—JANICE (not looking up, typing): Don't forget you're seeing Mr. Ellroyd in ten minutes.

—LAWRENCE: I know.

Pause.

—LAWRENCE (calmly, without moving his arms): Chris, bring me that letter from the tray, could you?

Chris smiles. He brings the letter to Lawrence. Then he sits in his chair and waits.

Lawrence opens the letter and reads it. There is a long pause.

—CHRIS: What do they say?

—LAWRENCE (smiling): They can't have me.

—CHRIS: Why ever not? How extraordinary. I mean . . .

—LAWRENCE (musing): I knew this would happen. I felt it. (Pause.) I wonder . . . it can't have been the Opera. (Pause.) They don't mention it. (Pause.) That could be taken either way.

—CHRIS: But what do they say!

—LAWRENCE (reading): 'Dear Mr. Gurney, since our Creative Director's return from holiday certain facts have arisen which have necessitated a drastic revision in our staff commitments. As a result I very much regret we have after all no vacancy at present . . .' And so on and so on and so on. Try in six months. Excellent test. Any other Agency be more than pleased. Yours sincerely. *Sincerely!*

—CHRIS: You must try again. Obviously they've lost an account or whatever happens to Advertising Agencies. Try another firm.

—LAWRENCE (smile): Why?

—CHRIS: Why? How do you mean? Because . . . I mean all the things you said this morning. The . . .

—LAWRENCE (half to himself): You know, I don't think I could. (Pause.) I'm almost relieved. (Pause.) The funny thing is, I don't think I even want to.

Pause. The telephone rings. Janice lifts it.

—JANICE (into telephone): Yes.

She replaces receiver.

—JANICE: Mr. Ellroyd's secretary says will you go up right away. His meeting finished early.

Lawrence slowly stands up. He holds one clenched fist to his mouth. Pause.

—LAWRENCE: I'm frightened. (Pause.) I hadn't thought of that. Obviously they've communicated. I should never have challenged them. Never.

—CHRIS: Oh, don't be silly. How could they communicate? Why should they? That never happens.

—LAWRENCE: You don't understand. They're both Jews. Ellroyd's half Jewish, Palmer the Creative Director is a Jew. Business is riddled with it. It's a system.

Pause. He walks to the middle of the room.

—LAWRENCE: I've never been sacked. I suppose it's something—or odd—to have reached the age of forty-two without being sacked.

—CHRIS: They won't sack you. Don't be silly, Lawrence. You're just upset.

—LAWRENCE: The odd thing is I feel I'm watching myself. A very odd feeling. (Pause.) This isn't happening to me at all.

—JANICE (unconcerned): Well, what do you want me to do with these, then? Do you want me . . .'

—LAWRENCE (shouting): Shut up! Get on with your typing. Don't talk to me.

He walks rapidly to the door. Stops.

—LAWRENCE: I'd better face the music. Take over, Chris. Don't worry I'll be all right. (Pause.) I wish I'd never challenged them. They're far too powerful. I must have been mad.

He goes out. Janice looks after him and shrugs her shoulders at Chris.

—JANICE: He said it. I think he's screwy all right. What a performance! I pity his poor wife. No wonder she left.

*   *   *

Dissolve through to Ellroyd's office. Ellroyd at his desk. Lawrence comes through the door near him, from the secretary's office.

—LAWRENCE: Sorry, sir. I had some things to attend to.

He stands in front of the desk, a prep school boy.

Ellroyd comes round from behind his desk and sweeps Lawrence before him into the corner of his office, where a black leather banquette along the two walls half surrounds a low, black marble table.

—ELLROYD (during this action): What weather! And they say snow tonight. What?

He sits Lawrence down at one end. Lawrence gives an impression of helplessness. Ellroyd sits next to him, rather close. He pushes an open cigarette box between them.

—ELLROYD: I shan't beat about the bush, Gurney. Lawrence. Bush! A bird in the hand is worth two in the bush. I always think there's a joke there, but I'm damned if I can find it. Ha ha a ha.

He is putting Lawrence at his ease. He produces a piece of paper on which he has made some notes.

—ELLROYD: I don't know how much you know at Management level about the position we are in at this moment?

—LAWRENCE (pause): In general terms? Not very much, I'm afraid.

—ELLROYD: Our profit figures are still not bad by British standards, but they've been declining very gradually for eight years. A pattern has set in. We've got to reverse it.

As you know, our Chairman Mr. Bolton retires in a year. As Vice Chairman I've been put in charge of reversing this pattern.

He stops. Sits back and looks at Lawrence. Change of tone.

—ELLROYD: Do you know what I want of this firm Lawrence, what I want this business to be, to *do*?

—LAWRENCE: ?

—ELLROYD (positively): I want it to sing. I only want singers here. By singers of course I mean those with ambition. Men with fire in their bellies. I want this to be the most ambitious, singing concern in the whole of Europe—and I intend to see that it is. Anyone without ambition—out! Psssst! Kaput!

There are some drops of sweat below Lawrence's nostrils. Ellroyd consults his paper.

—ELLROYD: I've already started some reforms, some big, some small. We're after new markets—aggressively. We'll be diversifying. But I've come out at a lot of odd things. Did you know we had an age problem? Age-wise, we're top heavy. Over half the firm are fifty-five or over. With reduced recruiting this will become marked. Old firms don't sing Lawrence. I intend to do something about this. It will be tough on some, but that's the nature of the best.

Ellroyd pauses. Looks at Lawrence. Change of tone.

—ELLROYD: I don't need to tell you what this means. The age problem affects the Board as well. There'll be vacancies. We may need one or two outside people, but I intend to see our boys get a fair crack of the whip. Where there's fire in the belly under forty-five, there's going to be a *very* fair crack of the whip. Of course, it will need a certain ruthlessness. It will mean responsibility. But that's meat and drink to a singer.

Pause. Ellroyd consults his paper.

—ELLROYD: Tell me, Lawrence, what's Robert Glenny like?

—LAWRENCE (pause): Bob Glenny?

—ELLROYD: Does he sing? Has he got it? How does he score?

—LAWRENCE (slowly): Bob's not ambitious. He's—what shall I say? Competent. He does a good job. He knows Packaging and Design. But (pause) well, I was promoted over him. He's never appeared to mind. But he's very good.

—ELLROYD (decisively): He'll have to go. He's (consults notes) yes, fifty-five. Rising fifty-six. Typical of our problem.

—LAWRENCE (shocked): But he's been here years. He's coming up for full pension.

—ELLROYD: Precisely. People hanging on for their pension don't sing.

—LAWRENCE: But you can't sack him just for that. Can you?

—ELLROYD (impatiently): Good heavens, Gurney, where's your fire! I thought I'd explained. It's not sacking. It's redundancy. He won't lose much. He'll get his pension as it stands now. It will be a bit smaller than full pension, of course, smaller than if we'd been able to keep him on. We'll give him a handshake—six months' wages. That's a lump. Skilfully invested it could bring his income practically up to full pension. There'll be others in the same boat I can assure you of that. He'll get another job. What's the market?

—LAWRENCE: At fifty-six? I don't know in Packaging and Design. I (pause) I understand it's not too easy in Advertising.

—ELLROYD: Competent. Knows his job. He'll find something, perhaps less well paid. He'll have to save. I said it would be tough, but as I said—that's the nature of the beast.

Now, Lawrence, I want you to tell him.

—LAWRENCE: Me?

—ELLROYD: Yes. As I said, it will mean increased responsibility. It will mean ruthlessness. But the rewards are there.

—LAWRENCE: But . . . I mean . . . You want me to tell Bob? To sack him? To make him redundant? Today?

—ELLROYD: I don't care when you do it. The sooner the better. Gurney—you have fire in your belly I'm given to understand. You surely don't need time to consider a thing like this? Eh? I thought I'd made it plain. I want singers here. Non-singers —out. Eh?

—LAWRENCE: Yes. Of course.

—ELLROYD (rising, smiling): Fine. Now, I must get on. Excellent. We'll have more talks, Lawrence. Do you know that terrible army expression? Really vulgar. Stay with me and you'll fart through silk. Awful expression. Now I must get on.

He claps Lawrence on the shoulder and, as it were, serves him like a tennis ball out through the other door of his office. He turns back to his desk.

—ELLROYD (calling): Who or what's next?

—SECRETARY (from next door): B Division. Sales Manager. Mr. Ritson.

—ELLROYD: Get him up. We're ahead of schedule.

*   *   *

Cut to darkness. Gradually our eyes become accustomed to it. The camera is facing away from the window into a small office. It is the office of Miss Hockin. We are now able to see by the light from the street lamp, from the glow of evening London. Nothing seems to have changed in Miss Hockin's office. The camera holds for approximately two minutes. It is very silent.

The camera now tracks forward. It passes through the shut door. It tracks with ever-increasing speed. Down stairs, along corridors, more stairs (this is in fact the reverse movement of its progress towards Miss Hockin's office in the morning). A lift door opens and shuts, empty except for one person: Charlie is at his exercise. Other familiar shots. We are outside Lawrence's door.

*   *   *

Cut to inside Lawrence's office. He is at his desk, arms straight, palms flat on the top.

—LAWRENCE: Chris and Janice, leave the office, will you? Chris, tell Bob I want to see him, will you?

—CHRIS: Yes. OK. (He rises.)

—JANICE: What's up.

—LAWRENCE: Leave the office please. Quickly.

They get up and go out. Lawrence lifts his hands to his head. He lowers them swiftly as Bob comes in. He stands up.

—BOB: Was there something, Lawrence?

—LAWRENCE: Sit down, Bob. Yes, there was.

Pause. They sit down.

—LAWRENCE: I'm not quite sure how to say this.

—BOB: Say what?

Bob begins to fill his pipe.

—LAWRENCE: Oh Lord—I wish I hadn't got to say this, Bob. I've got some bad news, Bob. I'm afraid it's going to be rather (pause) tough.

—BOB: Well, unless me whole family's been murdered in their beds which I'd be more likely to know than you, it can't be that bad. I've been in this business too long to be fussed by panics, Lawrence. What do they want; a whole new line in containers by tomorrow morning or something?

—LAWRENCE (pause, slowly): I've just been talking to the Vice Chairman, Bob. Mr. Ellroyd. God knows why he chose me. He explained about the position of the firm. It's doing badly. I can't exactly explain. They having to make people redundant, Bob. A lot of people. (Pause.) I'm sorry, Bob—but he asked me to tell you that you're one of the people.

—BOB: What?

—LAWRENCE: I'm sorry, Bob. I wish I could do something. I did my best. (Pause.) I can't think of anything to say.

—BOB: What do you mean, redundant? That I'm no good at my job?

—LAWRENCE: No, no. Nothing like that. They're having to cut down all round.

—BOB: What do you mean, then? I've got to move to some other department? Where do they want me to go? Not Manchester or something?

—LAWRENCE: They ... (Pause.) Bob—it means you'll have to get another job. It should be quite easy. And there's a handshake —six months' pay. (Pause.) I wish I could ...

—BOB (pause): You mean I've been sacked?

—LAWRENCE: They're having to make a lot of people redundant. I expect I'll be redundant soon.

—BOB: Sacked.

He stares at Lawrence. He puts his pipe on the desk and stands up. He has gone very red. Pause.

—BOB: I shan't go. They can't do that to me. I'm nearly fifty-six. I've been with this firm twenty-nine years. What right have they to sack me? What have I done? Go on—I ask you. What do they think I've done?

—LAWRENCE: It's not that, Bob. It's nothing to do with that. I told them—you were very good. You're far better than I am.

—BOB: It's nothing to do with you. It's nothing to do with this man—who is he?—Ellroyd. I shall go to my own Director. I shall go to Mr. Hines. He's our Director. I'll go to Mr. Bolton if necessary. He only joined the firm a few years before me. Who does he think he is—Ellroyd?

—LAWRENCE: You can try, Bob. I'll support you all the way. I think it's wicked. But Ellroyd is the Vice Chairman, you know. And Bolton's retiring soon; Ellroyd will probably be Chairman then. I expect Hines will be retiring soon.

—BOB: What about my pension? I was aiming for full pension. I'll lose that.

—LAWRENCE (quickly): You'll get the pension you're due. And six months' salary. That's quite a lump. Properly invested it will bring your income nearly up to full pension.

—BOB: What do I know about investing? I can't invest. I've worked here for twenty-nine years; I was planning to stay till I was sixty-five for a full pension. How about that?

—LAWRENCE: I thought you had some private means, Bob.

—BOB: Private means? What do you mean?

—LAWRENCE: £5,000 a year or something coming.

—BOB: Who told you that?

—LAWRENCE: Janice said you'd something. Some expectations or something.

—BOB: Oh that. That's just a hobby, something to pass the time. A game. The latest lot's pyrites anyway. (Pause.) No, this is criminal, that's what it is. I've never been late. I've a good sickness record. I do my job. We should've had a Union. I've always said that. My dad thought it was a step up. But I . . .

He stops and stares at Lawrence. He picks up his pipe and points it at him.

—BOB: What did you do? What did you say to this Mr. Ellroyd?

—LAWRENCE (spreading his hands): I told you, Bob. I told him he shouldn't do it. I told him you were a really good Package and Design man. I did my best—honestly. (Pause.) They'll probably sack me next.

—BOB: They won't sack you. Sack you? You're their class. You've got education. Of course they won't sack you. (Pause.) I'd've liked to have heard you. I can imagine it. You were scared stiff. You got the promotion, but I'm more professional than you. I'm a professional. I've done this job for twenty-nine years. I'd've never suggested a border of arses for one thing. Not on your life. You'd have never heard me suggest a thing like that. A border motif of arses indeed!

—LAWRENCE: What?

—BOB: Oh, I know it was a joke. But what a joke. Not a very professional joke. A border of arses.

—LAWRENCE: What on earth are you talking about?

Bob sits down again and stares at the pipe in his hands. There is a long pause. Lawrence grimaces, looks down.

—BOB: I'm sorry, Lawrence. I didn't mean that. Actually, we had a good laugh over it. I didn't want your job, as you know. It's just I don't know what I'm going to do.

—LAWRENCE: You'll get another job easily enough, Bob. You'll be snapped up.

—BOB: At fifty-six? Don't you believe it. And I don't want another job. I like coming in here. I know my way around. (Pause.) I was looking forward to another few years . . . my pension. I'll have to discuss it with Dad. (Pause.) And Dad. He's eighty—I have to support him you know. I've got two boys—eleven and thirteen—I was planning . . . What's he like, this Mr. Ellroyd?

—LAWRENCE: I don't know. Not pleasant.

—BOB: Do you think I could go to him? Explain the circumstances, about my dad, the two boys and so on?

—LAWRENCE: You could try, Bob. Quite honestly I don't see much hope . . .

Long pause. Bob sucks his pipe. He stands up.

—BOB: I'll have to work this out. Thanks, Lawrence, you've done your bit. You've stood by me. (Pause.) Don't spread it around till I've fixed something up, will you? (He begins to move to the door.) I'll have to talk to Dad about it. (Pause.) I may not take it lying down you know. (He turns at the door before going out.) Thanks, anyway, Lawrence.

Lawrence looks after him for a moment. He stands up and walks to the door.

He walks along the corridor and up the stairs (camera close on him). He walks purposefully, his face expressionless. At the fourth floor he turns aside to the lavatory. There is a notice saying 'Principals' on the door. Automatically, Lawrence turns away. But after a few steps his face suddenly contorts with rage. He turns back and pushes roughly into 'Principals'. It is identical with 'Gentlemen' downstairs. The same drab echoing dripping grotto. He stands, expressionless again, at the urinal.

He goes out (the camera following all this closely) and stands by the lift. He presses the button. It arrives empty and Lawrence steps in and presses for the top floor. He arrives, walks out and makes for a door at the end of the corridor. Although we do not know it, he is retracing exactly the route taken by him and Chris that morning.

It is dark and windy on the roof, cold. The rain is falling steadily. Lawrence walks across to the parapet, pauses, then swings his legs over and sits on it. The camera is about ten yards behind him, so that he is in silhouette, his long, thinning hair blowing in the wind, the rain visible against the lights of London.

The camera tracks in slowly until it comes up level with Lawrence and we are, as it were, sitting beside him.

Because one sees less, the noise of the traffic becomes more noticeable at night. The lines of buses, taxis, cars, lorries, pour across from Fleet Street down the Strand, hurry across Waterloo Bridge and into the underpass, or stop, then divide up the Aldwych and into the Strand. A succession of small races which are no sooner started by traffic lights than they are stopped by them. Nearly all the buildings have lights on behind their windows, lights in offices. There are some theatre lights up the Aldwych. We can see lights across and reflected in the river; almost make out the Battersea Power Station through the rain.

The camera tilts forward a little towards the street below. If you were to fall, or jump, you would land on, or perhaps hit and bounce off, a balcony which runs round the block three floors down. But only a small effort would be needed to make sure you missed it and fell clear the whole way.

The camera now looks directly down. The pavement and road

111

are eleven storeys (184 feet) below. The traffic is stopped at the lights. Now it begins to move.

*　　*　　*

A series of cuts.

Very quick, the Thumb Man lifting the bottle to his mouth and replacing it in the drawer. Camera behind him.

Jessie in her and Cyril Wells's office, humming. She is playing out some small fantasy. She puts on her spectacles, adjusting the ribbon, and reads a letter. She throws back her head and laughs lightly, aloud. She tears up the letter and throws it gaily into the waste-paper basket. She makes an expression of reproving herself, of resuming seriousness, and settles to a sorting task, humming.

Charlie. He is sitting in the chair in one of the hallways beside a lift.

The Gentlemen's on the second floor. A small quick man, thirty-six, with a superficial resemblance to Hitler comes in. He stands at the urinal and abruptly twists his head sideways on to his shoulder. When he has finished, he glances swiftly round to see if there is anyone there, then makes a surprisingly violent, convulsive movement, half shake, half shudder. He does up his fly buttons, then crosses his fingers and giving three short, loud whistles, darts both hands towards the urinal. He spits three times into the urinal, then runs rapidly on the spot, repeating the whistles. He goes out in rather a sly manner, looking sideways and walking with small, camp steps.

We are outside in a hidden between/behind buildings area, in a cul-de-sac. The camera is in front of a small, run-down café called Luigi's which caters for—taxi-drivers? all-night porters? sewage workers? waiters? It is snowing. Standing in the snow, which melts as soon as it lands, soaked, his face streaked with dirt, is Mr. Bolton. He is looking to the right-hand top corner of Luigi's Café, where a square extraction shaft comes out of the wall and disappears up into the darkness. He makes a note on one of the sodden plans he is carrying, then walks briskly off towards the opening of the cul-de-sac.

*　　*　　*

Cut to Ritson's office. Martin is sitting alone in it, smoking a

112

cigarette, looking at the snow which can just be seen falling outside the small, high, grimy window.

The door bursts open and Ritson rushes in. He is flushed.

—RITSON: I'm off. That's it—the buggers can lump it.

—MARTIN: Have they given you the sack?

—RITSON: Not quite. But the writing's on the wall. I know the signs. That bugger Ellroyd. Thank Christ I had that drink before I went in. I was just too quick for him. He couldn't pin me down. Now—first thing is another drink.

He puts his hand into the torn paper carrier bag beside him, takes out a three-quarters-full bottle of Spanish Burgundy and has a long pull at it.

—RITSON: Have some.

—MARTIN: Not at the moment.

Ritson puts the bottle on his desk and pulls his chair next to the filing cabinet. He opens the top drawer and takes out three files.

—RITSON: First thing is to cover our tracks.

—MARTIN: *Our* tracks?

—RITSON: Well, my tracks. But I'm afraid some of yours may get a bit blurred in the process. Don't worry, I'll see you don't get blamed.

He starts to go through the first file.

—RITSON: Whew! That won't do at all. Oh dear no.

He tears up a piece of paper and throws it into the tin waste-paper basket. Pause.

—RITSON: God, I feel randy again.

—MARTIN: I know—you could have a horse. What about what you said after lunch?

Ritson sits back, tearing up three letters and throwing the pieces vaguely towards the waste-paper basket.

—RITSON: Well, it's no good is it? You can't alter. I know myself, but self-knowledge never stops you doing anything; it just means you know you're going to do it.

I think I'll go back to being a Rep. The faery power of un-reflecting fucking. I met Pam like that, I think I told you. It's quite true what they say about sex and Reps you know. The number of randy women you just wouldn't believe. They just sit there among their Omo packets with their knickers off waiting for you to come. And when I say *come* . . . (Makes a face at Martin.) It's part of the job. Here it just interferes. I'm not good at an

office job, anyway. I'm too restless. I'll go back to being a Rep.
But of course the great problem is where. Some of the boys think
you get more sex in the country because they don't have it so
often. But there's others who say the town because they get a taste
for it. I don't know. It's a difficult problem. Academic. Scholastic
really. Someone should do a thesis on it.

He laughs and takes another enormous swallow from the
Spanish Burgundy. Then he lays the file across his knees and sits
musing, a bit drunk. Martin watches him.

—RITSON: All that's wrong with England, you know, is
parents don't love their children. Sex and loving children. You
never hear someone say about a Spanish father 'He loves his
children.' You do about English parents. That's pretty odd don't
you think? 'He loves his children, she loves her children,' as
though it was something extraordinary. *All* Spanish fathers *and*
Italian fathers love their children. Does that mean Spanish men
and women are more sexy? Or have more sex? I don't know.
Probably does. Except they're Catholics—poor buggers.

He takes another drink and more files. He begins to go through
the files faster and faster.

—RITSON: These are bloody ghastly. I haven't looked at them
for ages. (Pause.) This is no good at all. The lot'll have to
go.

He gets up and goes through into a small room off their office.
He comes back with a sack. He pulls his chair closer to the filing
cabinet and takes out the files one by one. During the rest of the
dialogue he rips through the contents of each file and stuffs the
papers into the sack. He rips with abandon and pleasure, even
appetite, like someone pulling down old wall-paper or some
hungry animal grazing. A remnant of office routine remains,
however, in that he returns each file, with the shreds of letters,
charts and records, to its proper place in the cabinet.

—RITSON: You know I've often thought of starting an Agency:
Introductions with a View to Fucking. I might do that.

—MARTIN: They've practically done it. Some of the small ads
you see nowadays more or less say that.

—RITSON: Have they? I knew it would come. No-one's
thought of my name have they? That's the point.

—MARTIN: Could I have a drink?

Ritson pushes the bottle towards him. Martin drinks.

—MARTIN: You might have difficulty with the advertising.

114

—RITSON: Do you think so? I thought you said they'd more or less started. Anyway, I see the world becoming very much more permissive. Minister of Sex. You know—a caption in the papers: 'Enjoying the late September sun, some couples spend their lunch hour fucking in the park.'

Pause.

—MARTIN: The Fuck.

—RITSON: What?

—MARTIN: A new dance called The Fuck.

—RITSON (laughing): That's it. Exactly. Anyway, that's what my Agency will be called, *Introductions with a View to Fucking*.

Pause. Picks out a bit of paper.

—RITSON: Look at this. Nil Return. Nil Return. Nil Return. Christ knows what the buggers *do* with their time. Well, *I* know what they do—but honestly.

He takes another drink from the Spanish Burgundy, which is now almost empty. He stops ripping to briefly scan another piece of paper.

—RITSON: You know, London is a very randy city. Very randy.

—MARTIN: What are you looking at?

—RITSON (absently glancing at the paper): Nil Return. Have you noticed that in summer the exhaust from cars sometimes smells of sex.

—MARTIN: No.

—RITSON: Well, it does. (Pause.) Pam will be waiting for me. I've finished this more or less.

He gets up and puts back the last of the files. He moves his chair back to the desk. He picks up the telephone.

—MARTIN: I thought you were going home.

—RITSON: A line please. (He dials.) I told Pam to wait unless I rang. Her sister's with the children. (Pause.) Angela? Look, darling, I shan't be home tonight. (Pause). I know, darling, but I've got a meeting with the Reps and then I've got to get the twelve-thirty to Manchester. (Pause.) Kiss the children for me. (Pause.) All right. 'Bye-'bye, darling.

He replaces the receiver and sits staring past Martin, vacant, glowing.

—MARTIN: Guilt?

—RITSON: No. Not yet. Not now. I will be. It's just a cross I'll have to bear. (Pause. He laughs.) A cross the shape of a prick.

115

(Pause.) No, I was thinking of Pam lying in bed at the Regina. (Pause.) Regina—what a name!

He stands up, picks up the Spanish Burgundy and finishes it. Then he puts on his mackintosh and picks up the sack.

—RITSON: I'll dump the body somewhere. In the river. I'll be in some time tomorrow to finish clearing up. Finish the bottle.

—MARTIN: Thanks.

—RITSON: I'll bring one in tomorrow. Well—I must be off.

—MARTIN: Have a nice time.

—RITSON (grins): My balls are boiling already.

He swings the sack over his shoulder and walks out. Martin stares after him, then grinds his cigarette end round and round in the ashtray.

*　　*　　*

Cut to Cyril and Jessie's office. Jessie filing; Cyril going hither and thither.

—CYRIL: Where's my board? I must have that board. Have you seen the board, Jessie?

—JESSIE: Mislaid it, have we?

She rises, puts on her spectacles.

—CYRIL: I'm already late. I can't remember if he said today or tomorrow. I may have made a note on the board.

—JESSIE (peering, bending): There's some fey, some little imp . . .

—CYRIL (pouncing): Ah! Now . . . no . . . I can't stay searching. I must get down there at once.

He hurries towards the door.

—CYRIL: Jessie—could you possibly . . .?

The rest is cut off by the closing door.

—JESSIE: Tst-tst. Now we'll *never* know . . .

She settles her spectacles.

*　　*　　*

The camera cuts to Cyril hurrying through the corridors. There are other people but the camera, now hand-held, is thrusting through and past them to keep up with Cyril, rather as an athlete is always kept in camera running through a town.

Although there is a sense of drama and speed (Cyril actually

116

begins to resemble a Marathon runner, ten miles out and going strong), there is also a sense of his having taken, taking, the longest possible route. We seem to follow him for hours.

He arrives at Ritson and Martin's office. Knocks. Hurries in. Stops.

—CYRIL: Oh. Ah. Sorry, Mr. Ritson. Didn't mean to barge in. As a matter of fact there is—that is, Mr. Ellroyd has—I'm afraid it must be getting pretty urgent——

—MARTIN: Mr. Ritson isn't here. He's gone home.

—CYRIL: Oh my God! Gone home? What on earth am I to do? He can't have gone home. You're sure?

—MARTIN: What do you want?

—CYRIL: Ah yes. Now, where are we . . .

He shuffles through the board.

—CYRIL: Good Lord—here's the confirmation of Bee's memo. Mrs. Dugdale's memo. Thank God. That's quite a relief, to be off the hook.

He goes through papers.

—CYRIL: Yes. Here we are. A report on Reps' Commissions he sent Mr. Ellroyd three weeks ago.

—MARTIN: You can look in the files if you like. I'm afraid you're unlikely to find anything. Mr. Ritson's been reorganising. In that cabinet behind you.

—CYRIL: Ah, thanks. It'll take a bit of time—Recent Memos I imagine. Or Reps' Commissions. But I can stay late. I once fell asleep in my office here you know. Woke at three thirty. I couldn't get out. Oh I got a lot done . . . Cleared (pause) quite (pause) a (pause) backlog. (Pause.) Quite . . .

He has been going through the files with increasing bewilderment. Faster and faster. Each reveals the same raped interior.

—CYRIL: There's been some mistake.

—MARTIN: Try the next drawer, or the one under that. As I said Mr. Ritson's been carrying out a reorganisation. You *might* find something.

Cyril pulls open the next drawer and starts to look through it. He begins to get frantic. He pulls the bottom drawer bodily out of the cabinet and across the floor. A few shreds of letter and memo flutter about.

—CYRIL: Reorganisation? This is the work of a madman. There's nothing here. Look! Nothing! A maniac has been at work. Oh God.

117

—MARTIN: It's true Mr. Ritson had a fairly comprehensive clear out. I think he's decided to resign.

—CYRIL: Oh my God. It's happened.

He seizes his hair and sinks into Ritson's chair.

—CYRIL: The worst has happened. The Vice Chairman. What'll he say? What will I say? I shall be sacked. Oh Lord.

—MARTIN (pause): I don't see that it's anything to do with you. I should simply explain what has happened.

Cyril doesn't answer. At last he raises his head, his jaw set, face white. He gets up and begins to gather the files into a heap.

—CYRIL: I'll just have to work on it tonight. See what I can make of this nonsense.

A fragment of paper falls from one of the files.

Cyril grabs it and clips it to his board.

—CYRIL: I may be able to piece something together. It's the only way. Show willing.

Pause. The pile of files is now considerable.

—CYRIL: It's a real nonsense. I'll be up all night.

He picks up the pile and staggers to the door.

—MARTIN: Your board. I'll put it on the top.

He balances the board on the top file. Cyril is now almost completely hidden. Martin opens the door for him.

—CYRIL: Thanks. I'll be back for the rest in the morning.

He goes out.

*　　　*　　　*

Cut to Mr. Bolton's office. Bolton, again in a complete change of clothes, is standing in the middle of the room. There is a glass of whisky in his hand. Miss Sturt is standing in the door of her office.

—MISS STURT: You've got to see her now, Mr. Bolton. She's been on the telephone all day. She's had this appointment since twelve forty-five, when you put her off.

—BOLTON: Show her up. Show her in. I'll see anyone.

Miss Sturt goes out. Mr. Bolton sips his whisky and swaggers over to one of the abstract paintings on his wall. He looks closely at it, takes another sip of whisky, then steps back holding up his thumb and squinting at a black whorl in the upper left hand corner. He grunts.

The door behind him opens and Bee bursts into the office.

She is, to use her own words, in full war paint. Orange lips,

118

mascara, shaded, foundationed, powdered, scented, rouged . . .
the lot. Mr. Bolton holds out his arms.

—BOLTON: Bee, darling! You look lovely. Join me in a drink.

—BEE: Oh, thank God I've found you Bolly. I should have
gone mad. I can't tell you what I've been through. It's been too
awful, since this morning . . .

—BOLTON: Here I am. Calm down, dear. Have a drink. I'm
sorry about this morning.

—BEE: Oh, this morning. That's nothing. It was this afternoon. I could hardly bear it.

—BOLTON: Well, start at the beginning. What about this
morning?

—BEE (impatiently): Oh, nothing. That was just Jack. About
my hot plates satisfying my needs. Nothing.

—BOLTON: Satisfying your needs? That's not nothing. Come
on, Bee, I should have . . .

—BEE (interrupting): You *must* take this seriously, Bolly. The
most appalling thing has happened. Do you know Mr. Braine?

—BOLTON: Braine? An excellent man. First-class. Ambitious.
Got the layout of these buildings at his finger-tips.

—BEE: So he's been lobbying you, has he? I thought he would,
the scheming, nasty . . . I may tell you he's not all he seems. He's
a *fiend*. A bullying, scheming *fiend*.

—BOLTON: What's he done?

—BEE (pause): You know my office? My lovely office? You
know the years I've spent perfecting it; the little touches, the
trouble.

—BOLTON: You certainly have a very nice office. So you
should. You've been with us a long time.

—BEE: You know my really lovely old desk?

—BOLTON: I can't say I remember your desk precisely. I know
you have a desk of course but . . .

—BEE (sweeping on, voice rising): He's tearing it from me.
He's forcing me to have a new desk, a horrid new desk. He's got
this huge new desk—all shiny, no patina, no charm—this great
gross object outside my door.

—BOLTON: But . . .

—BEE (voice rising): I won't have it. I'll resign if I have to
have it. He won't listen to me. I was never consulted.

—BOLTON: But surely, Bee, a nice new desk. Wouldn't it be
rather nice? New.

119

Bee stares at him, unbelieving. Then, drawing a deep breath, she bursts into tears. She falls on to Mr. Bolton. He just manages to put down his whisky and hold her up. He pats her and comforts her.

—BEE (through sobs): Don't you understand? ... all these years ... my poor little faithful old desk which I love ... they all ride roughshod over me ... you're my only hope ... don't you remember? ... Bolly ... please stop them ... I'm only a woman ... it's blocking the corridor ... I have to climb in and out ... oh I can't bear it, I can't bear it, I can't bear it.

—BOLTON: Quietly now. That's all right. Here have my handkerchief, your eyes are running. You needn't have a new desk. No-one in the firm must be forced to have a new desk. Of course you needn't have a new desk. Now have a drink.

—BEE: You'll stop him? Now.

—BOLTON: Well—I can hardly believe *I'm* necessary. Tell him yourself.

—BEE: He won't listen to me. Will you do it?

—BOLTON: All right, if you insist.

—BEE: Now?

—BOLTON: Now, if you like. All right.

—BEE: Ring him up.

—BOLTON: No, I'll send him a note. (Calling.) Sheila.

Miss Sturt appears.

—BOLTON: A memo to Mr. Braine. 'Please arrange that Mrs. Dugdale keeps her old desk.' I'll sign it in the morning. (To Bee.) There.

—BEE: Oh, you're wonderful, Bolly. I knew you'd save me. You wonderful man. Where's my mirror. I must look a sight. You've saved my life.

She works on her face.

—BOLTON: Now, have a whisky, Bee. Join me in a whisky.

—BEE: Not just now, Bolly. I've got to fly.

—BOLTON: I'll have one, then.

He goes over and pours himself a large whisky, a small measure of soda.

—BOLTON (lifting his glass to her): This is to cleberate, Bee. I've pulled something off. There's spunk in the old dog yet. I'm on the takeover trail again.

—BEE: You're wonderful, Bolly. God knows what'll happen when you go. You're my idea of a man.

—BOLTON: Sure you won't have a nip?

—BEE (as if recollecting herself, moving to the door): I can't, Bolly. What am I *doing* here? I've asked a few people round. I don't know what comes over me. None of them knows each other. A writer, a couple of artists—and my *aunt*! And a few more. But sometimes that works don't you think? It'll be a question of Instant Thumbnails all round. I must fly.

—BOLTON: Keep it under your hat. I don't want anything to leak till it's out.

—BEE (advancing): Oh, Bolly—you're my idea of a man. I'm so grateful. You're so wonderful.

She bends to kiss him. With amazing speed, Mr Bolton puts down his whisky, seizes her by the buttocks, pulls her to him, stands on his toes and thrusts his tongue into her mouth. Bee responds.

—BEE: Mmmmmmmm (breaking away). Oh, Bolly! After all these years!

She runs gaily to the door. Turns.

—BEE: And you're still my favourite yummy man. 'Bye!

Mr. Bolton watches the door close. He finishes his whisky and goes to get another.

—BOLTON (calling): Sheila.

—MISS STURT: It's on five thirty, Mr. Bolton.

—BOLTON: One letter, Sheila?

—MISS STURT: It's on five thirty, Mr. Bolton.

—BOLTON: It's quite short. I'll sign it in the morning. You can type it in the morning.

Now, it's to the Manager of Luigi's Restaurant. Where's that plan? I wrote the address on the plan. It must be in the suite. Half a minute.

He walks towards the door behind his desk.

* * *

Cut to Cyril and Jessie's office. Cyril is sitting looking at the heap of files.

—CYRIL: He'll have to sack me. He'll have no option. It was a direct, personal directive. If I'd gone at once this wouldn't have happened. (Pause.) Finding Bee's memo counterfoil may help. I'll bring that up.

—JESSIE: Shot at dawn? Off with his head? Oh, surely not.

121

Surely that's not like our lord and master?

—CYRIL: Funnily enough, now that the worst I've ever imagined—worse than I've ever imagined—has happened, I feel nothing. I feel quite numb. (Pause.) My toes are tingling. That's all.

—JESSIE: We've had a busy day.

—CYRIL: It's not over yet. I'll have to sort through this nonsense. It'll take me all night.

—Jessie: Take it home, Mr. Wells. Do it in the parlour, sitting round your own fire. Your good lady wife can bring you hot bovril.

—CYRIL: Perhaps you're right. God knows . . . No. I'll do that. Where's my board? Help me get some string round them. They weigh a ton, even if they are nearly empty. That Ritson—he must be a maniac.

—JESSIE (helping him tie): Wouldn't like to meet *him* on a dark night.

*   *   *

Cut to Lawrence's office. Peter is standing behind Lawrence's empty desk watching the snow. It is now falling fast, an endless swift flow of large flakes streaming down, hypnotic, an impenetrable curtain. Chris and Janice at their desks.

—PETER: It's so *cosy*. It always reminds me of my prep school like this, sitting on a radiator and staring out of the window. The prospect of some ghastly game being cancelled tomorrow. Snow falling on all those little boys tucked up in bed, warm and snug.

He turns to Chris and Janice.

—PETER: And here we are—snug in our little cosy offices. I don't know what Lawrence *means*—I really don't. (Pause.) Where is Lawrence?

—CHRIS: I don't know. He just disappeared. (Pause.) I'm a bit worried about him. He's been in an odd mood all day.

—PETER: I expect he just went home early.

—JANICE: Yes—to throw more furniture down out of the window, I expect.

She gets up, puts the cover on her typewriter and puts on her coat.

—JANICE: It's after five thirty. I'm off.

—PETER: Why don't you like him?

—JANICE: I don't know. He get's my goat, that's all.

She does up her coat and puts a scarf over her hair.

—PETER: Your goat?

—JANICE: Yes, dear—my goot (imitating).

—PETER (mildly): Don't mock the affected, dear—they can't help it.

Janice goes out slamming the door.

—PETER: Oh dear, I seem to get her goat too. (Pause.) I suppose I do say goot as a matter of fact.

—CHRIS: Well, I must be off.

—PETER: Yes. I'll have to leave the bicycle. I think I'll take a taxi. That's another pleasure—a taxi in the snow.

THE DEPARTURE

CUT to sound and visual wild track of the office being abandoned. Men coming out of a Gentlemen's. Secretaries leaving in a bunch. Doors swinging. Notices blowing on the boards as people hurry past. It is as though the office will explode or sink if they don't get out in time.

Cut to a lift. This is, or should be, Charlie's moment. He stands by the automatic buttons, holding the door open. Then he presses the ground floor button.

Dissolve through to the lift some moments later. People press into the lift. Charlie is forced back from the door. Gradually he is trampled out of sight at the back.

Dissolve through to the lift again. It is filling swiftly. Charlie steps out to let people in (we recognise some of them—the Executive, the man who resembled Hitler). The lift becomes full, too full to hold Charlie. The doors close in his face. He stares irresolutely at the closed doors, then presses the button to recall the lift and shuffles slowly towards the stairs.

Cut to the Thumb Man going down the stairs. Camera follows him from behind. People pass him. One speaks.

—MAN: 'Night, Bill.

—THUMB MAN: 'Night. Good night.

He goes down the stairs further than the hall into a basement area. A back door brings him out into a small street in which there is a pub, The Bunch of Grapes. The snow is falling hard. He stops in the street and turns up his collar (the camera all the time behind him). He walks towards the pub. A man comes towards him, walking fast. The Thumb Man stops.

—THUMB MAN: Hi, Bob. Coming for a quick one?

—MAN (pausing): Not tonight, Bill, thanks.

—THUMB MAN: I think I'll just step in for a quick one. Had rather a heavy day. Got to unwind, eh? Ha ha ha ha.

The man hurries on. The Thumb Man goes into the pub.

Cut to a bent back (it might be Bolton or Ellroyd or one of the other Directors) inclining, subsiding, into a Rolls-Bentley.

Cut to Jessie standing in a bus. She is trying to read a woman's magazine, despite the swaying and jogging. Her small woollen hat is covered in glistening drops of melted snow. She is wearing mittens.

Dissolve through to office workers walking through the Embankment Gardens towards Charing Cross Underground. The camera is one of them, moves with them, does not concentrate on them.

We can see that the snow, though falling swiftly, melts as soon as it lands. The pavements and roads are shining wet.

We are at the bottom of Villiers Street, where it turns right. The camera is on the bend. And now we hear a very strange noise that can be heard on any day of the year at this time and this place. It is the soft, insistent sound of feet, the murmuring of hundreds, thousands of feet. No-one speaks. Mostly—and especially tonight as it is snowing—they look down. And some trick of echo or enclosure magnifies and at the same time muffles the tapping, shuffling, scraping of the feet. It is hushed and hurried, like people going to the Last Judgement. Like a death march.

The visual counterpart of this sound is the endless flow of faces. The camera now tracks towards the Underground to concentrate on these.

This sequence should last four or even five minutes. Nothing is so eloquent of The Office than the faces of its returning workers.

Cameras can be set up and hidden at bus stops or Underground stations, at Charing Cross or Oxford Street or the Bank or Holborn, at any of the great whirlpools into which the millions of returning workers are sucked each night. Hidden—or not hidden. The faces are oblivious of each other and of their surroundings. They certainly won't notice a camera or two.

During this sequence we recognise only two people. One is Cyril, barely able to carry his files. The other is Lawrence. The camera rests on each just long enough for them to register.

At length, despite the apparently random recording of the camera—the close-ups, the blurred waiting ranks dissolving through to more blurred, waiting ranks, long shots of heads, from the back, going down the escalator, descending tussocks, faces—it becomes plain the camera has a direction again.

It is moving back through the faces, against the tide. There are fewer people. The camera is outside Holborn (or the Temple, or

125

Charing Cross or Bank . . .). It is moving through fewer and fewer people, back to the office.

*   *   *

The camera is drawn to the office quite slowly by a series of dissolves.

We arrive at the large glass and bronze doors of the main hall. They are closed. Dissolve through to the hall, and at the same time the sound is cut off. There is dead silence. The camera floats up the stairs at head height, disembodied, a ghost.

We reach the third floor. The camera, as though searching, looks into the Gentlemen's, soundlessly flushing.

We move down the corridor. All the doors are open, all the lights on, but everyone has left, draining the office, sinking like the sea through sand and like the sea leaving it exactly as it was before.

Or not exactly as it was. We pass Bee's door. On her desk is her notice: *'On no account is this desk to be moved or touched.'* Bob Glenny has left his bag of gold behind.

Suddenly, startlingly, two cleaning women appear at the end of the corridor, pushing vacuum cleaners. They are talking and laughing, though we hear nothing. They separate, each taking an office on opposite sides of the corridor.

The camera starts to track down this corridor towards the stairs. And now we hear, for the first time in the film, music. It is very quiet, only just audible.

The camera moves faster. It is following a definite route: into another corridor, up some stairs, left at the top, along another rather worn corridor, another flight of stairs, dingier, steeper. The music grows louder.

We are in the corridor outside Miss Hockin's office. A cleaner is walking down it carrying a dustpan, broom and mop. The camera slows, following her.

She stops outside Miss Hockin's door. She opens it. Turns on the light. We follow her in.

She picks up Miss Hockin's chair and puts it on the desk. She puts her dustpan on the desk. Then she takes the broom, which is a large one, and begins to sweep out the office.

The music grows gradually louder all the time.

The cleaner comes level with Miss Hockin's filing cabinet.

126

Bending down she takes hold of the bottom drawer and with a single movement pulls it open. Then she plunges her brush into the drawer and begins to sweep it out.

Immediately, an explosion, a fountain, of tiny pieces of paper bursts from the drawer, a jet of confetti. Oblivious, the woman continues to brush it out. The office rapidly fills with a swirling, paper snowstorm.

The music reaches its climax. The camera pulls back towards the window. It is driven back by the pieces of paper. It draws back, through the window, out into the night, so that for a moment we don't know which is paper and which snow.

The lights of the office, of all the offices, are below us, growing smaller. We draw back and back and back until they merge together, indistinguishable, until the screen is filled with whirling specks—snow, lights, paper.

MAIN CHARACTERS

Lawrence Gurney—forty-two, head of a Packaging and Design Group.

Miss Hockin—fifty-two. A secretary.

Charlie—lift-man.

Woodrow Bolton—sixty-four. Retiring Chairman.

Bob Glenny—fifty-five. 2 I/C Lawrence's Packaging Group.

Cyril Wells—thirty-four. A Progress Section man.

Janice—nineteen. Lawrence's secretary.

Peter Villiers—thirty. Executive in Specifications.

Bee Dugdale—about fifty. An Executive.

Geoffrey Ritson—forty-five. B Division Sales Manager.

Miss Sturt—fifty. Bolton's secretary.

Chris—about twenty-five. Lawrence's assistant.

Bill—the Thumb Man—an Executive.

Jack Ellroyd—forty-six. Vice Chairman.

Martin—twenty-four. Ritson's assistant.

Jill, Christine, Sue—secretaries.

Jessie—about sixty. Cyril Wells' assistant.

Diane—telephone operator.